AF488559

MAMM'S THANKSGIVING PLAN

Amish Romance

HANNAH MILLER

Tica House
Publishing

Sweet Romance that Delights and Enchants!

Copyright © 2022 by Tica House Publishing LLC

All rights reserved.

No part of this book may be reproduced in any form or by any electronic or mechanical means, including information storage and retrieval systems, without written permission from the author, except for the use of brief quotations in a book review.

Personal Word from the Author

To My Dear Readers,

How exciting that you have chosen one of my books to read. Thank you! I am proud to now be part of the team of writers at Tica House Publishing who work joyfully to bring you stories of hope, faith, courage, and love.

Please feel free to contact me as I love to hear from my readers. I would like to personally invite you to sign up for updates and to become part of our **Exclusive Reader Club** —it's completely Free to join! Hope to see you there!

With love,

Hannah Miller

**VISIT HERE to Join our Reader's Club and to Receive
Tica House Updates:**

https://amish.subscribemenow.com/

Contents

Chapter One

"Isaac Yoder asked me to go for a buggy ride with him," Ruth Lantz said, letting out a dreamy sigh as she rocked in one of the chairs on Lucida's front porch. "I can't believe it's taken him nearly two years to get the courage to ask me."

"Well, men can be that way." Lucinda shrugged, picking at a stain on her apron. In the middle of baking an apple pie, she had dropped some of the filling. Despite immediately using a damp rag to wash it away, it had still left a sticky darkened spot. "Not that I would know," she added, shaking her head.

"You haven't gone on a single buggy ride for just one reason," Ruth teased, her dark locks peeking out from her *kapp*. "You won't give any suitors the time of day. You've had plenty of offers, Lucinda—some of them were fine men, too."

Lucinda gazed at her best friend curiously. She couldn't think of a single man who had asked her out who seemed like a good option. It was not that she was so picky, either—there was just ... no chemistry with the men who asked her.

"None of them were the right one," Lucinda finally replied, shrugging her shoulders. "The right man will sweep me off my feet, and there'll be a ... a zing." Her voice was wistful and distant, recalling some of the books she had gotten ahold of during *Rumspringa*. She didn't read those sorts of books anymore.

But sometimes she still thought of them and the romance that exploded between the main characters in the story.

"Well, I don't know how you can determine such a thing without ever even giving them a chance." Ruth laughed, leaning back in the chair. "I think you might be running out of men here in Rock Point."

"Maybe the right one for me isn't *in* Rock Point," Lucinda countered. "There are more men than just those here. Maybe the right man for me hasn't moved here yet."

"Maybe." Ruth shrugged. "I'll pray that *Gott* brings the right one along for you, Lucinda. I think you deserve the very best."

"You do, too," Lucinda replied, giving her friend a warm smile. "I think *Mamm* is starting to worry about it, though. She's always talking about how I'm twenty-two now, and that by this age, she had already married *Daed*—and had Jack." She rolled her eyes, letting out a frustrated grunt. "I don't know how I'm ever going to make her happy."

"By getting married," Ruth pointed out, bursting into laughter. Lucinda giggled along with her, even though it bothered her that Ruth was right about it. Her mother would be overjoyed if Lucinda would start courting someone instead of always turning them down.

She looked out across the small front yard, where their house in town was situated right in the middle of everything. Her family had used to live out on a farm, but when her father had passed away nearly five years ago, her mother had given the house to Jack, and moved to town with Lucinda. It was easier to live there in town, but Lucinda couldn't help but miss the peace and quiet that came with the farm. She had already decided that whomever she married—they would have to come with a farm.

No more living in town for me.

Lucinda was certain the man she was looking for probably didn't exist, but it didn't keep her from dreaming him up in one way or another.

"Do you think Isaac Yoder is a good choice?" Ruth turned to Lucinda, grabbing her attention again. "He's very handsome," she added, her cheeks reddening.

Lucinda smiled. "I think he's nice enough. I've heard he works a lot though," she said blandly, thinking of the Yoder's construction company.

"I don't see that as being a bad thing," Ruth countered, furrowing her brow. "A man who is busy with his hands is a man who doesn't have time to get himself into any mischief—that's what my *mamm* says."

"Well, your *mamm* is much wiser when it comes to men than I am," Lucinda joked, picking at the stain on her apron again. "I'm afraid I might not ever get any wiser when it comes to men and those sorts of things."

"You will in time." Ruth's voice was reassuring, though Lucinda wasn't sure she agreed.

Before Lucinda could continue the conversation, the front door opened and her mother, Marge, stuck her head outside. "Lucy, it's nearly dark, and I need to speak with you about something before I turn in for the night."

Lucinda sighed at the use of her nickname but nodded. "All right, *Mamm*. I'll be in as soon as I tell Ruth goodbye."

"Make it fast," Marge warned, giving her a knowing look. Her mother had reason to throw a threatening expression, as it wasn't uncommon for Lucinda and Ruth to forget they were supposed to be saying goodbye, getting lost in conversation all over again.

"She sounds serious." Ruth giggled as soon as Marge disappeared back inside the house. "I probably should get going, too—my *mamm* gets worried when I wait to walk home until after the sun goes down."

"I'll see you tomorrow then," Lucinda said, pushing herself up from the chair. "I suppose I should see what my *mamm* wants to chat about."

"You'll have to fill me in on it tomorrow," Ruth replied, also standing to her feet. She stretched her arms above her head, letting out a yawn. "Have a good night, *Lucy*."

"Oh, stop," Lucinda quipped, rolling her eyes. "You know I don't like that nickname."

"I know," Ruth teased as she headed down the porch steps. "I'll see you."

"Bye." Lucinda waved and headed into the house. As soon as she shut the door behind her, she turned to see her mother, sitting at the table waiting for her. A pang of worry hit her in the chest. "Is something wrong?"

"Well, I don't think it is, myself," Marge answered, giving Lucinda a smile. "But we do need to have a conversation. Things are fixing to change."

"Oh," Lucinda said, pulling out a chair and taking a seat at the table. She wasn't sure how to feel about her mother's odd demeanor, and she caught herself growing more anxious as she waited for her to continue.

"As you know, my own *mamm* isn't doing as well," Marge began, placing her hands gently on the table. "And I'm going to go to Pennsylvania to take care of her."

Lucinda hesitated, trying to wrap her head around what her mother was saying. "So, does that mean I'm going with you?"

Marge sighed, shaking her head. "There's not enough room at her tiny *daadi haus* for both of us, and so I have taken it upon myself to makes plans for you as well."

"*Oh...*" Lucinda's voice broke off, taken aback by her mother's frank confession. "And what plans are those?"

"Well, as you know, my best friend Doris Schrock, writes me nearly twice a week ever since she moved off to Beacon's Point. She and I have discussed our plan for quite some time, and we feel it's finally time—and *Gott's* will that we move forward with it now."

Lucinda's stomach tightened, having *no* idea what her mother was talking about—but it was making her feel on edge. "I don't know what you mean."

"She has a son, Jeremy, who has yet to court anyone. He's nearly twenty-four years old and still hasn't married—can you believe that? He took over his *daed's* farm when he passed away, and he also works with leather, so he's artistic in the same way you are with your quilts. His mother and I have felt for a long time the two of you were the perfect match, but we were waiting on *Gott*," she said with a smile, her eyes bright.

"You'll move to the Schrock farm next week right before I leave for Pennsylvania."

Lucinda's mouth gaped, her eyes stretching wide. "Are you serious, *Mamm?*" She gasped. "I can't marry a man I don't even know." Her heart nearly exploded in her chest at the mere thought of it; she was deeply troubled.

"Now, Lucy," her mother said softly, obviously trying to calm her down. "There's no need to be worked up—there's nowhere else for you to go…We think this is perfect."

Lucinda shoved herself back from the table, her upset morphing to anger. "I will *find* somewhere to go. I'm not going to be forced to marry. That's not even fair for you to ask me to do something like that." She stormed out of the kitchen, thundering up the stairs to her bedroom. Throwing herself onto her bed, she began to cry defiant tears. She wasn't sure if she was angrier about having to leave Rock Point, or if she was just heartbroken that her mother expected her to marry someone she had never even met. There was no way she was going to do such a thing—she'd have to come up with another place to stay.

I'm not going anywhere.

Chapter Two

Lucinda was up before the sun peeked through the window, unable to lie awake any longer. She hadn't slept well the entire night, still deeply troubled by the idea of marrying Jeremy Schrock. There was no way she was going to go to Beacon's Point—not if there was any way for her to avoid it.

"Please *Gott,* let this work out," Lucinda mumbled as she dressed for the day, carefully putting her hair up in a bun. She was hoping to slip out of the house before her mother could ask where she was headed, so she couldn't do anything to stop her. Lucinda was certain her mother already knew she would be planning to try everything she could to stay in Rock Point, but still.

It was just easier if Lucinda *didn't* have to explain where she was going.

Taking a deep breath, she slipped out of her bedroom and crept down the stairs. Thankfully, she didn't have any morning chores to do right away, and her mother's job at the bakery meant Lucinda could get away without making breakfast. Sliding her boots on and heading out, Lucinda winced as the door creaked, the sound seeming to pierce the quiet around her.

She wasted no time heading straight to see Ruth, whom she knew would already be up. Her best friend lived just outside of town on her family's farm, so they were always up before the sun. Her boots crunched along beneath her, and the morning was a bit chilly, cutting through her light coat. Lucinda wrapped her arms around herself in an attempt to make it a little less unpleasant.

I can't believe Mamm is really doing this to me.

Her stomach tightened into knots as she thought about it. It felt as though her mother had betrayed her. She was just passing her off to get married as a means of solving the issue of where Lucinda would stay if she went to Pennsylvania. It was frustrating—and upsetting.

"Good morning, Lucinda," Ruth's father called out to her as she walked across the front yard of the family's farmhouse. "I'm surprised to see ya here so early."

"I guess I'm just out and about a little earlier than normal," she answered, trying her best to sound as cheerful as possible. "Do you know where Ruth is?"

The slight, gray-bearded man seemed to ponder the question for a minute before answering. "I think she's around back cleaning out the chicken coup. We're trying to ready for Hannah to arrive this next week or so."

"Oh, I see," Lucinda said, heading around the back of the house where the chicken coup was located. Hannah was Ruth's older sister and lived in a town over with her husband and baby. It wasn't uncommon for her to come and visit, so Lucinda didn't think much of it. She turned the corner of the quaint white farmhouse, her eyes landing on Ruth, holding a shovel inside the large, caged area.

"You're out early," Ruth called to her as she looked up.

"That seems to be what everyone is saying to me this morning." Lucinda laughed softly, shaking her head. "You'd think I was lazy or something."

"I guess that depends on who you ask," Ruth teased, pausing to wipe the sweat from her brow. "You look perplexed though —is everything all right?"

Lucinda let out a heavy sigh, her shoulders sagging. "Hardly. My *mamm* told me last night that she wants to move to Pennsylvania to take care of my *mammi*."

"Oh," Ruth said, her voice dropping. "Does that mean you're going to move, too?"

"Sort of," Lucinda answered, her stomach flipping. "She wants me to move to Beacon's Point to live with the Schrocks—and marry Doris's son, Jeremy."

"*Nee...*" Ruth's eyes went wide, and she leaned her shovel up against the chicken wire. "You can't be serious?" She wiped her hands on her apron and slipped out of the door.

"*Mamm* is *very* serious about it—she says it's *Gott's* will," Lucinda added with a grumble, shaking her head. "I don't know how it could possibly be true, though. How can I marry someone I've never met?"

"It happens more often than you'd think," Ruth pointed out, shrugging. "Though I just find it surprising that your *mamm* would do such a thing. Have you prayed about it yourself?"

"The only thing I've been praying for is to find a place to stay here," Lucinda answered, folding her arms across her chest. "I can find a job here—or sell my quilts. I just need to find a place to stay..." Her voice trailed off as she held Ruth's eyes, hoping that she would catch the hint of just what she was getting at.

And she did.

"Oh, Lucinda," Ruth said with a sigh. "I wish you could stay here, but Hannah is moving home. I found out about it when I got home last night."

"What? Why is she moving home?" Lucinda asked, struck by the surprise. "Don't they have a nice farm?"

"Well, they did, but Levi decided to sell it." Ruth rolled her eyes. "He's planning to buy another farm out in Pennsylvania—but they can't move there for another four months. So, they're moving here for the time being." Her voice was tinged with an annoyance that would've made Lucinda laugh if the circumstances were different.

And if it hadn't ruined her hope to live with her best friend.

"Well, I suppose you'll have a very full house with them all living here," Lucinda commented, her voice full of disappointment. "There won't be a spare room, will there?"

"*Nee.*" Ruth shook her head. "And I have to share a room with Susie."

Lucinda rubbed her fatigued eyes. "I guess I'll have to go ask Jack if I can move in with him and Rachel."

"In that *tiny* farmhouse with their three *kinner?*" Ruth questioned, her brows furrowing. "Where in the world will you sleep?"

"Maybe the sewing room?" Lucinda offered with a shrug, though she knew it was a stretch—but she was still going to ask. "I have to try, Ruth."

"I suppose so," her friend replied, though her face was mirroring the defeat Lucinda was already feeling. "You'll write me if you do move, right?"

"Of course," Lucinda answered. "Though I sure hope it doesn't come to that."

"I can give you a buggy ride over to Jack's if you want," Ruth offered, giving her a reassuring smile. "That'll save you a long walk, and Rachel was making us a few pies anyway."

"That would be much appreciated, thank you." Lucinda smiled, though she was hardly feeling anything positive. Her stomach was still tight, worrying pulsing through her body.

"Absolutely not," Jack answered with a grunt, folding his arms across his chest. "If *mamm* says she wants you to go to the Schrock farm, then I'm not going to go against it. Besides, Rachel's already on me about adding onto the house. She's not going to give up the sewing room. I just don't think it's a *gut* idea."

Lucinda let out a frustrated groan. "But don't you understand, *bruder*? How in the world am I supposed to marry a man I've never even met."

"I completely understand what you're saying, Lucinda," he said, his face full of sympathy. "But that doesn't change the fact that I'd be going against *Mamm* and my own wife. I'm not going to do that. Also, I trust *Mamm* if she says that it's *Gott's* will. She's a wise woman of faith, Lucy."

"It's not fair," Lucy whined, shaking her head. "I don't see how it could possibly be *Gott's* will for me to move to Beacon's Point."

"Well, I've met Jeremy Schrock," Jack said with a shrug. "He's a fine man, and he works very hard. I can see why *Mamm* would see him as a *gut* fit for you. I don't really see anything wrong with it. You surely haven't been doing anything on your own to find a husband."

"I don't want to go," Lucinda snapped, raising her chin defiantly. She knew she was acting childish about it, but the point she was making didn't feel so out of order. "How am I supposed to know if he's the right one if I've never met him? I want to fall in love."

Jack's face contorted in what Lucinda thought might be understanding, and he let out a sigh, scratching his thick red beard. "Well, I *do* see what you're saying. But what if you go, and just tell *Mamm* that you don't want to get married right away. She can't *force* you to marry Jeremy."

Lucinda considered what her brother was saying and grew silent for a few minutes. If she agreed to go, but not get married, she could possibly find another job there, and then move away from the Schrock farm once she got settled. The change of scenery wouldn't be the worst thing. After all, there wasn't really anything keeping her there in Rock Point, and she could potentially meet the right man in a different town.

Someone who was *not* Jeremy Schrock—not that she even knew for sure that she wouldn't like him. It was just the simple fact that he was being forced on her that made her already make up her mind it wouldn't work between the two of them.

"I don't know of anyone hiring around here, either," Jack continued at Lucinda's silence. "Rachel has been asking around town for her younger sister, Mary, and there hasn't been a single job opening come up anywhere that has any sort of housing available. There's a couple of farms hiring, but they're fit for a young man, not a woman like you, who spends her free time quilting."

Lucinda pursed her lips, glancing up at the sun rising in the sky. "I guess that just further makes the point that I will *have* to go to Beacon's Point." She sighed. "*Mamm* will be elated."

Chapter Three

"Did you hear me, Jeremy?" Doris Schrock, his mother, demanded, her voice coming out quite sternly. "Lucinda Gundy will be here in two days."

"I heard you," Jeremy grunted, working his swivel knife delicately in the dampened leather hide. He kept his eyes focused on the floral pattern he was outlining, careful to keep the blade at the proper angle. The last thing he wanted was to gouge out the leather.

"Well, could you put that knife down for just a moment, so we can talk about your soon-to-be wife?" His mother was beginning to sound more and more annoyed with him with every word, but he shrugged it off, having no intention of hearing her out.

Because he wasn't planning on getting married any time soon.

She could bring whomever she wanted to their house, but that didn't mean he had to agree to do anything about it. His mother and her best friend might think they had concocted an infallible plan, but Jeremy didn't have to participate in it.

I'm a twenty-four-year-old adult.

I don't have to do anything I don't want to do.

"I don't know why you have to be so difficult about this—it's a *gut* thing. You've never even courted a woman before. It's time for you to settle down and have a family. Sarah's already having her second child."

Jeremy rolled his eyes at the mention of his younger sister. "That's great for Sarah, *Mamm*. I don't see why I need to rush off and get married." It wasn't that he didn't want to get married exactly, it was just he didn't have the time to put into a marriage. Besides, women were complicated, and some of his friends complained about their wives.

It sounded like a bigger hassle than it was worth.

Running a farm and leather shop was enough of a strain—no need to add anymore stresses to his life.

"Lucinda Gundy is a beautiful, smart young woman. She sews lovely quilts, and her hair is the color of wheat and her eyes the color of the blue sky."

"So, she's got green hair." Jeremy chuckled, shaking his head. "I don't think that's such a great quality, *Mamm*."

"Oh, stop it," Doris snapped, her voice tinged with irritation and a little amusement. "I mean it's a golden light blonde. You've always said you like blonde hair."

"I don't recall ever saying that," Jeremy grunted, though it was true. He did think blonde hair was beautiful, but it was only because it was different from his dark, coffee-brown hair. He'd never actually seen the color blonde his mother was referring to.

But that didn't matter.

Lucinda Gundy could be the most beautiful woman in the world, and it still wouldn't change his mind about marrying her. There was something about it being forced that made it very unappealing. Thankfully, it wouldn't be hard to avoid the mess considering how much he worked.

"She'll be here in just a couple days," his mother repeated herself. "I've readied everything for her. I figure she can stay in Sarah's old room. You'll be nice to her when she arrives, won't you?"

"Sure," Jeremy answered with a shrug, though internally he didn't plan to have to be anything to her. Again, he was busy enough to not interact with her at all.

"I think she's nervous. Marge said she didn't take the news as well as she had hoped, but it's because she doesn't want to marry a man she's never met—and I suppose I can't blame her for that. But *Gott* will reach her, just like He will reach you, too. You'll both see that it's *Gott's* will in time."

"All right," Jeremy said with a sigh, trying to let all of his mother's words go in one ear and out the other. He was hearing her, just not truly listening. Besides, the whole thing felt a lot more like *her* plan than *Gott's*.

"Aren't you just a little bit excited?" Doris questioned him, leaning against the wall of the tack shop attached to the house. "I thought you'd be relieved you didn't have to go on the hunt for a wife at all. You always tell me that's the reason you haven't courted anyone—that you just don't have the time."

"Well, that's the truth," Jeremy answered flatly. "And I don't see why we have to keep talking about all of this. I'll meet her when she gets here, and that'll be that. I'm not going to force her to marry me, either," he added, finally looking up from his work to meet his mother's gaze. "I don't want to be married to someone who doesn't want to marry me."

"She's just a little shy," his mother reasoned, shrugging her shoulders. "She hasn't met you yet, but when she does, she'll be head over heels—just like all the other girls in town."

He rolled his eyes, completely unconvinced. Not only was his mother *somewhat* wrong, but she was *very* wrong. He hadn't shown interest in any girls, and none had seemed interested in him either. His mother was always thinking he was the best catch for a woman—and he *did* have a farm and leather business, but that didn't seem to matter. He was tall with broad shoulders, towering above most of his peers by a solid six inches. Therefore, being taller than all the men made the disparity between himself and women even worse. It made him feel awkward around them, even despite having a sister.

I look like a giant.

"How tall is Lucinda?" he asked, only a little bit curious. Jeremy looked back down at his leather work to keep from seeing the giddy grin on his mother's face he was certain was there.

"Her mother says she's almost five-foot-four," Doris answered him, her voice matter of fact. "So, I supposed that makes her about average height."

"And over a foot shorter than me." Jeremy grimaced, shifting uncomfortably in his seat. It was even more of a reason to avoid her—he already knew he would be awkward around a woman of her height. Not to mention, he wasn't the best conversation starter. His mother was chatty, able to talk to anyone—or anything. No one had to talk back for her to keep talking away.

"A woman is supposed to be shorter than a man, you know," Doris pointed out, folding her arms across her chest. "I don't know why you think you're too tall."

"I don't think I'm too tall," Jeremy shot back, jumping on the defensive. He was pretty sure his mother knew all of his insecurities. However, there were plenty of others that bothered him too—like how he had never kissed a woman before. Most of his friends seemed to catch onto that one very quickly, especially during *Rumspringa*—but not Jeremy. He'd never even held a woman's hand before.

"You're a *gut* man, and you'll make a fine husband," his mother continued, her voice bright and excited. "I think it'll be nice to have another woman around, too. It sure is lonely here now that Sarah has moved out and started her own family. I was thinking we could build a *daadi haus* in the back for me once the two of you are married. I'm sure you'll want to get started on having a family."

Jeremy's knife slipped at the mention, cutting an ugly streak across the middle of one of the flowers. He let out a frustrated grunt and shook his head.

Well, I'll just have to cover that somehow.

He was pretty good at covering up the flaws in his work. In fact, he believed that the best leather patterns had a flaw of some degree—that was what made them artistic. If every single one was perfect, then they'd all be the same.

"Can't you imagine having a strapping young son to follow you around? To learn the same things your *daed* taught you?"

Jeremy's heart clenched with grief. "It'd be nice," he mumbled, trying to push away thoughts of his father. It had only been a few years since he had passed away from the flu, and Jeremy was reminded every day when he worked the farm alone just how much he missed him.

He wouldn't have forced me to get married to some girl I don't know.

Except for the fact that his father probably actually would have, if it was what his mother wanted or what he thought to be *Gott's* will. His mother was a wise spiritual woman, and there was no doubt she always prayed diligently about things, never rushing into a decision without fervent prayer first.

But in this situation...

It just didn't seem like *Gott* could possibly want Jeremy to marry a girl he had never met. He'd only ever met her older brother, Jack. He was a fine enough man from what he could tell—and he didn't even doubt that Lucinda was probably a nice woman. It was the fact that he hadn't been able to find the right one in Beacon's Point, so what were the chances of the right one being his mother's best friend's daughter?

Chapter Four

Lucinda wearily packed up her things, her stomach churning with nerves. It wasn't a long drive from Rock Point to Beacon's Point, but the idea of riding in a car with a stranger for two hours was a bit unnerving. There were plenty of Amish folks who rode in cars every day to get to their construction jobs, driven by the *Englisch* who worked with them. It wasn't that Lucinda thought there was anything wrong with it per se, it just unnerved her.

Cars moved a lot faster than buggies.

Back during *Rumspringa*, she had always been too nervous to go along with her other friends in cars. It was part of the reason she and Ruth had become best friends. Neither of them were a fan of vehicles.

"They'll be here to pick you up in about thirty minutes," Marge commented, peeking her head into Lucinda's room. "I know you're nervous, but I promise you, it'll be a wonderful experience."

Lucinda felt a lump growing in her throat as she folded the last dress for her suitcase. "I hope so," she mumbled, her voice barely above a whisper. "You'll be a long way away."

"I'll write to you every week." Marge smiled, entering the room and walking toward Lucinda. "I know this is a big change for you—and I know it's overwhelming. Give yourself some time to settle in, but I have no doubt you'll find Jeremy makes a fine husband."

Lucinda gritted her teeth, not sure anymore what to think about any of it. She still had no intention of marrying Jeremy —though she hadn't told her mother that. All she had said was she would go but would *not* marry him as soon as she arrived. She wanted plenty of time for a courtship and plenty of time to do things the proper way. Her mother seemed a little disappointed—but only a little. For the most part, she was happy Lucinda had given up her fight about not going at all.

There was knock on the front door, echoing through the house and up the stairs, interrupting Lucinda's thoughts.

"I bet that's Ruth." Her mother smiled. "I know she wanted to see you off. I'll go let her in and send her upstairs to see you."

"Thank you, *Mamm*," Lucinda muttered, blinking back a few tears. She was already feeling homesick, not even having left yet. It was a surreal feeling, and despite being irritated with her mother for even putting her in the situation, that was where her hard feelings ended. If anything, the anger had worn off to just being...*sad.*

"Oh, honey," her mother said before leaving the room, rushing to Lucinda to wrap her in her arms. "Everything will be fine." Her voice was reassuring as Lucinda's tears began to fall freely, soaking her mother's pale pink dress.

"I'm terrified," Lucinda choked out, admitting some of her deep hidden feelings for the first time. She had been defiant on the outside about it all at first, but the closer she got to the hour of her departure, the stronger her fears had grown. "What if they don't like me?"

"Of course, they're going to like you," her mother murmured, patting Lucinda's back gently. "You're a lovely woman, and I have no doubt Doris and Jeremy are both going to not just like you, they're going to *love* you."

Lucinda sniffled, squeezing her eyes shut as more tears slipped down her cheeks. "I hope so," she mumbled, hardly able to believe that two strangers would take to her so well. "I just hope I don't talk too much."

"Well..." Marge laughed softly, pulling away from Lucinda slightly. "I have no doubt that you'll fit in just fine with Doris. She talks more than you and me put together times ten."

Lucinda giggled through the tears, comforted by the fact that Doris was such a good friend of her mother's. "Well, we should get along just fine—I'll go see Ruth now, I suppose. We've just left her out there waiting for me."

"*Oh,* poor Ruth," her mother exclaimed, rushing off and down the stairs.

Lucinda laughed a little and then grabbed her full suitcase, taking one last glance around her bedroom. It was bare and lonely, since she had opted to take the quilt she had made herself. It wasn't her best work by any means. In fact, it was one of the first she had ever made entirely on her own—but it would always serve as a reminder of home.

As she lugged her bag toward the stairs, she could hear Ruth and her mother chatting just outside the front door on the porch. Her heart clenched at the sound, realizing it would be the last time she heard anything of the sort for a long time. Her mother intended to keep the house and return to it, once Lucinda's grandmother was feeling better—or if she passed away. Lucinda tried not to think of that scenario.

But part of her did hope that her grandmother recovered quickly, so that maybe they all would be able to go back to normal.

"Lucinda," Ruth greeted her with a smile as she opened the front door to join them on the porch. "I am going to miss you *so* much."

Lucinda was moved by the tears in her best friend's eyes. "I'll miss you, too," she cried, fresh tears escaping from her eyes as she tugged Ruth into a tight embrace. "I don't know what I'll do without our visits."

"I guess you'll just have to write to me *all* the time," Ruth sniffled, holding Lucinda tightly. "I'll write you about everything that happens here, too, I promise."

"I'll do the same for you," Lucinda replied, releasing Ruth so she could wipe her tears away. "Everything will be just fine." She was repeating her mother's words, trying to say them enough times so she would believe them herself. "And good luck with Isaac. He's a nice man."

"Well, I'll have to keep you in the loop about it. We've only gone on one buggy ride, you know..." Ruth's voice trailed off, sounding a bit disappointed. Ruth looked away from Lucinda, and it was more than apparent that something was wrong.

"What's the matter?" Lucinda asked, reaching out to squeeze Ruth's hand. "Did something happen last evening?"

Ruth sighed, giving Lucinda a half-smile. "It actually was a lovely time, and he even held my hand—can you believe that? Holding my hand on the first buggy ride? I was *elated*." Ruth beamed, before her face fell. "But he hasn't asked me on a second ride. I just knew that he was going to mention it at the end, but he didn't. He dropped me off and then left."

"Maybe he didn't want to seem too eager," Lucinda's mother, who had been listening, chimed in. "Lucy's *daed* was like that at first in our beginning of courtship. I never knew if the man actually liked me, but once he got over his nerves, it was smooth as can be."

Lucinda watched as Ruth's eyes lit up. "You think that's all it is? I sure hope so—I had an amazing time. I just...I just don't want to be excited, only to be disappointed when he doesn't want anything more to do with me."

"He would be *crazy* not to court you," Lucinda drew out, placing her hand comfortingly on her best friend's shoulder.

"I have to agree," Lucinda's mother said. "You're a fine young lady."

"You'll have to write me and tell me all about it," Lucinda spoke up, her heart sinking at the distance that she would be putting between herself and her friend. "I'll miss our time together."

Just as the words left her mouth, a red SUV pulled up in front of the Gundy house, and they all turned to look. It wasn't uncommon to see *Englisch* motor vehicles parked in front of Amish homes as the Amish used them for long distances. However, the look on her mother's face told Lucinda that this was not just any vehicle.

This was the one coming to take her away.

"The woman driver's name is Lauren—she's a nice *Englisch* woman," Lucinda's mother said as the three headed toward the SUV. A middle-aged red-headed woman dressed in a long jean skirt and black t-shirt slipped out of the car, giving the three women a smile.

"Good morning," she greeted the women, her eyes bright and warm. "Which one of you is Lucinda?"

Lucinda returned the smile. "Me," she said, holding up a hand timidly. Some of the time, the Amish took a bus, and Lucinda had ridden on one with her mother once to visit her grandmother. It had been stale and stuffy, with a few people who made her uncomfortable...

So maybe a car ride wouldn't be so bad.

"I'll take your bags for you," Lauren offered, holding out a hand. "It shouldn't take us long to get to there—only about an hour and forty-five minutes."

Lucinda nodded, taking a deep breath, and handing the woman her two bags. She watched as Lauren placed them in the back of the car and then opened a passenger door. "I'm ready when you are." She beamed, that same warm expression on her face.

"Have a safe trip," her mother said, pulling in Lucinda one last time for a hug. Lucinda held back the tears the best she could.

"Write me when you make it to Pennsylvania," she choked out before releasing her and turning to embrace Ruth quickly. "I'll miss the both of you so much."

With that, she stepped away from them, sliding into the black seat of the SUV. It smelled of leather and pine, which happened to be a very comforting scent. However, the moment the car pulled away, Lucinda's chest began to ache for home, wishing she could just tell Lauren to turn the car around and go back.

Chapter Five

Jeremy pulled the buggy up at the gas station right outside of Beacon's Point, letting out a sharp nervous exhale. There was no reason for him to feel anything other than annoyed about picking up Lucinda, but sure enough, he was feeling more apprehension than anything else. He rubbed his eyes and scanned the parking lot. His mother had insisted on hiring a private driver to bring Lucinda to town and had also insisted that Jeremy pick her up from the gas station instead of having her brought all the way out to the farm.

Which meant a forty-five-minute buggy ride back.

It's just another part of her plan.

He shook his head in pure annoyance and leaned back against the bench. He was losing valuable time in the workday having to pick up Lucinda, and he had no idea why his mother had to conspire with her best friend and put him in such a predicament. It was like they *wanted* to make his life more difficult.

Jeremy glanced up, recognizing a familiar red SUV parking on the other side of the buggy. Lauren was a common driver for the Amish, and he had seen her around the town often. She had driven his mother to see some of her family as well as to see Marge Gundy, Lucinda's mother. Taking a deep breath, he exited the buggy, hopping down to greet Lauren, who was already climbing out of the car.

"How're you?" Lauren asked, giving him a smile. "There's just a couple bags in the back—I'll grab them."

"I can help you," Jeremy said, following her to the back of the SUV and grabbing two somewhat small suitcases. He was surprised to see that was all Lucinda was bringing—but maybe she didn't plan to stay there very long. With a shrug, he grabbed one in each hand, backing away as Lauren shut the back hatch. As it closed, he met a set of bright, sky-blue eyes.

Wow.

It took a moment for him to realize he was staring at a young, Amish woman, who he assumed was Lucinda. Her blonde hair peeked out from her *kapp* and his mother had been right, it was the color of golden wheat, beautiful beneath the light of the midday sun. He quickly tore his eyes from her, turning away to walk around to the other side of the buggy to stow the suitcases—taking the long way just to avoid looking at her.

I should probably offer to help her into the buggy.

Grimacing, he grabbed the money to pay Lauren and walked back around, handing it to her. "Thanks for giving Lucinda a ride," he said gruffly, nodding his head to her.

"Have a wonderful day, Jeremy," Lauren said, before adding, "You, too, Lucinda. It was nice getting to know you this afternoon."

"You, too," a timid, sweet voice said from beside him. He gritted his teeth at the way it made his chest stir ever so slightly. He kept his eyes trained on Lauren, who ducked into her car and drove away.

Leaving him stuck with Lucinda.

"I'm Lucinda," the sweet voice said, this time with an air of apprehension to it. "You must be Jeremy?"

"Yep," he answered, still not looking at her. He did, however, offer his hand to help her into the buggy. Much to his surprise, she didn't take it. Instead, she climbed into the buggy all on her own. A jolt of rejection seared through his chest, and he grunted as he walked around to join her in the buggy. It was clear she did not want to be here...

So then, *why* was she here?

As he stepped up, his eyes took in her silhouette, finding himself pulled to her perfection in the way she sat there. Her hands were folded neatly in her lap, and her eyes were focused out in front of her—not at him. Something about that bugged him, but he wasn't sure what.

Which left him feeling flustered.

He settled in beside her, noting just how small-framed she was sitting there beside his large frame. However, she didn't shrink away from him. She didn't do *anything*.

"It'll take about forty-five minutes to get to the farm from here," he found himself saying as he urged the buggy horse forward.

"That's quite a way," she replied, her voice distant and reserved as she spoke to him. "That's all right though. The drive went well—I've always been worried about riding in a vehicle for that long, but it wasn't so bad."

She's a talker.

He grunted, shifting in his seat beside her. "I see."

"Are you having a *gut* day?" she asked, finally looking over at him. He side-eyed her, meeting her gaze for just a moment. There was no doubt that she might actually be the most attractive woman he had ever seen, her dimples making his stomach flip—but like he had thought before, it wouldn't change his stance.

"I'm losing a lot of work time," he gruffly responded, leaning slightly away from her. "Never makes for a *gut* day when I'm behind."

"Oh," she muttered, her voice tapering off. His heart dropped at the tinge of disappointment in her voice, but he ignored it. There was nothing for him to feel bad about—he had made it abundantly clear that he had no interest in the plan Doris and Marge had conjured up.

He is not very welcoming.

Lucinda sat quietly beside Jeremy, stealing glances over at him the entire buggy ride. He was *very* handsome. It was a shame that his demeanor didn't line up with his looks. He was a tall, strong man, towering above her. His dark-brown hair matched his eyes that were the color of chocolate. He was much more attractive than the men back in Rock Point...

But not nearly as nice.

Ugh, and to think, Mamm *thinks I should marry him.*

She let out a sigh, and it came out much louder and more dramatic than she intended.

Jeremy's head snapped in her direction, and he raised an eyebrow at her. She ignored it and looked away out the window.

Please just get us there.

There was no doubt that she was going to have a very wordy letter to send to Ruth, telling her all about just how *miserable* this was going to be. Lucinda had already planned to find a job and another place to live there in Beacon's Point, but after meeting Jeremy, she was more certain than ever she wouldn't be staying any longer than she had to.

"We're here," Jeremy grunted some odd minutes later.

Lucinda gazed out the window, her breath catching as she took in the long winding driveway to a two-story white house at the end of it. The pastures out front were dotted with cattle and horses, and it was just as she had imagined the farm should look. As they started toward the house, the wheels creaked, and the hooves of the buggy horse crunched on the gravel. Her eyes went straight to the beautiful white porch, noting a woman standing there.

"Is that your *mamm?*" she asked, turning to look at Jeremy.

"*Jah,*" he answered her flatly, not even looking to where she was pointing.

All right, then.

As soon as the buggy came to a stop, she jumped out, hardly able to stand it any longer. There was *no* way she was going to be able to marry a man whom she couldn't ride in a buggy with for forty-five minutes. That was a sure sign that it wasn't going to work out.

Maybe I should write Mamm *and tell her right now.*

"Lucinda," the woman from the porch called out, snapping her back to reality. "I haven't seen you since you were a little thing." She came down the porch steps to greet her, her dark hair graying around her temples. "I'm Doris, in case you don't remember me," she said as she wrapped Lucinda in an embrace. "I'm so excited to see you."

Lucinda was overwhelmed as Doris squeezed her tightly, feeling all the warmth that Jeremy had lacked.

"Thank you," Lucinda murmured, not sure of what else to say. As Doris released her, Lucinda caught sight of Jeremy, carrying her suitcases up to the porch. He didn't even look over at her at all as he walked by.

He dislikes me.

"Let's get you settled in," Doris said, grabbing her hand and leading Lucinda up the porch steps and into the quaint home. It smelled of apple pie, which was comforting, reminding her of her own home. Doris led Lucinda up the stairs, to the first door on the left.

"This will be your room," she said, a smile on her face. "It was Sarah's, but I think it will work perfectly for you."

"Thank you," Lucinda said as she took in the warm room—minus Jeremy who was tossing the bags onto the bed. There was something homey about the way it was situated, the full-size bed covered in a brightly colored quilt. She would probably replace it with the one she brought, but still.

"I gotta get back to work," Jeremy grunted as he squeezed past Lucinda. She caught a hint of leather as he passed, and it caught her by surprise, drawing her in.

"You can take the afternoon off to spend some time with Lucinda," Doris called after him, turning back to give Lucinda a smile. "He'll warm up. He's just a busy man."

Lucinda nodded, thankful that Doris was so warm and welcoming—the total opposite of her son. It was just too bad she was a co-conspirator with her mother, putting Jeremy and Lucinda in the predicament in the first place.

Chapter Six

"Well, it's two weeks from Thanksgiving," Doris said, her voice sounding warm as she took a sip of her hot tea. "I don't know about you, but the holidays are my favorite time of year."

"Oh, they're definitely mine as well." Lucinda beamed across the table. She'd been living at the Schrock farm for nearly three weeks, and she had found herself settled in, though she was keeping her options open. After all, Jeremy was *never* around. He hadn't eaten supper with them but one time, and even then, he had left early, carrying his meal with him out to the leather shop.

She knew that part of his absence was because he was finishing up harvest and helping out other farmers in the community. It was an admirable thing, but she never told him that. In fact, she never actually told him anything. He never gave her more than a passing glance, and she had grown accustomed to it. It was clear that all the desire for a marriage was solely the responsibility of their mothers.

"You know," Doris said, a smile stretching across her face, "I have just missed having my daughter here at home for the longest time. Once she left, it felt a little lonely. Jeremy is a lovely man, but you can see how much he works—and I have to say, men just don't like to chat about the same things as we women." She reached across the table, taking Lucinda's hand. "I'm so glad that you're here, Lucinda. It's so nice having a young woman around again."

"Thank you," Lucinda murmured in reply, touched by the admission of the older woman. "That means so much to me," she added, before picking up her own cup of tea and taking a sip. The words also left her with a little guilt, mostly because unbeknownst to Doris, Lucinda had been quietly asking around town. It wasn't that she didn't like living there at the Schrock farm, it was just clearer than ever that there was never going to be a marriage resulting from her stay.

So why would she want to remain there?

"Now, I guess since you're going to town this afternoon, I thought you might be able to pick up a few things for me from the bakery—and I thought I might have Jeremy take you to town, if that's all right?" Doris suggested, her eyes lighting up and her face flashing with some sort of happiness at the mention of Jeremy taking Lucinda into town.

"Doesn't he still have some chores to do?" Lucida asked, hoping more than ever that he did. "I don't want to be a bother to him." That was the truth, too, she *didn't* want to bother Jeremy. Anytime she was, he was never very joyful to join her—and mostly just ignored her the entire time.

But also, this time she needed to check on a few of the job inquires she had made. There was a chance she might be able to find a job with a local mercantile and there was a nice furniture maker who was looking for someone to manage a lot of the record keeping and paperwork. Lucinda had been hopeful she could speak with them. After all, those were the only two jobs that had materialized in the slightest on her behalf. All the rest had been filled before she could even ask.

"He's already planned to take you into town," Doris said, a smile on her face. She was beaming at her own words, and *that* was the only thing she found frustrating about Doris. She was still *so* determined to tie her to Jeremy, though it was clear he wasn't interested.

And neither am I.

Though, the thought didn't feel like it was fully the truth anymore. Jeremy avoiding her completely did hurt her. However, she wasn't sure if it was because she thought he was a truly attractive man, or if it was simply because it hurt any time someone was that blatantly obvious about not wanting anything to do with her.

Which, in truth, had never happened before.

"You can just drop me off at the bakery and go about your other errands," Lucinda said to Jeremy, who had been starkly quiet the entire buggy ride to town. She was hoping she could be dropped off and forgotten about for a while—so she could check in on the job opportunities.

"Uh..." He hesitated as he pulled up alongside the bakery. "I suppose I can do that."

"Great," Lucinda said, not even bothering to look over at him as she jumped out of the buggy. "You can pick me up here when you're done," she called over her shoulder, heading right into the bakery to pick up the few loaves of bread that Doris had ordered.

"It's lovely to see you this morning, Lucinda," Rebekah, the bakery owner, said to her as she stepped through the doors of the small bake shop. The smell was comforting, and the shop was warm, wiping the chill right from Lucinda's body.

"It's good to see you, too," she replied, seeing that Rebekah, the middle-aged woman, was already setting her order up on the counter in a brown paper sack. "Do you know if they've filled the position over at the furniture shop?"

Rebekah nodded, a curious look on her face. "Why, I think Elijah Yoder took the position just yesterday. He's one of those that's really talented with that sort of thing. I think it was the best fit they could've asked for."

"That's wonderful," Lucinda forced out, not wanting to sound resentful. If there was someone else who needed the job more so than she, it wasn't right for her to covet their opportunity. She didn't want to be selfish; she just wanted to be able to move out of the Schrock's farmhouse.

There's no way any man will be interested in me if I'm living there, anyway.

She pursed her lips at the thought, bidding Rebekah goodbye at the bakery and heading out. Lucinda hadn't really thought about what other men might be in Beacon's Point who needed a wife, but she was certain that anyone might be better than Jeremy. He might look like the man of her dreams on the outside, but he was nothing but a brick wall on the inside. She walked quickly down the street, heading for the mercantile shop just a few blocks away. She didn't want to run into Jeremy, as it wasn't right for her lie about what she was up to. That was the one thing she hadn't done. Despite quietly searching for a job, she told herself that she would be honest with either of them if they asked her.

It was the right thing to do.

But if they *didn't* ask, there was no reason for her to tell them...

Her stomach tightened at the thought, not sure if it was the godly way of looking at things. But surely, *Gott* understood. Her mother was making her miserable by trying to arrange her marriage to Jeremy Schrock, and honestly, she was just praying that both women would recognize that their plan had been about *their* wills, and not *Gott's*.

"Can I help you?" a dark-headed man said from behind the counter of the mercantile shop as she stepped inside.

"I was just wondering if you had any job openings," Lucinda began, smiling warmly at the young man. He was handsome— not *Jeremy* handsome, but still handsome. "Rebecca told me last week you were looking to hire someone to work here in the store."

"Well, we were," he said, his smile turning to a frown. "But unfortunately, we filled the position. Now that harvest is over, there are a lot of men needing some seasonal work. We always try to hire as many as we can—helps them get a little extra through the winter."

Lucinda nodded, disappointment washing over her. "Thank you so much for your time."

"It's no problem at all," he said, but hesitated for a few moments. "Aren't you the girl who moved in over at the Schrock farm?"

She sighed, forcing a smile. "*Jah,* that's me. Lucinda Gundy."

"Well, it's *gut* to see a new face around here. What is your connection there?" His eyes held hers with focused interest, and she felt a jab of excitement, though it was very tiny.

"I'm helping Doris out around the house," she said with a shrug. "My *mamm* is her best friend. She sent me here while she's in Pennsylvania helping with my *mammi*."

"I see," he answered, taking a step from behind the counter. His brown eyes lit up as he moved closer to her. "It's a pleasure to have you here in Beacon's Point. You're more than welcome to come by anytime you'd like," he added, his tone taking on a warm, borderline flirtatious tone.

Just as she was opening her mouth to reply, the door opened, ringing the small bells attached to the handle. Lucinda saw the look on the man's face fall slightly, and she turned to see who was walking in.

Ugh. Jeremy.

There was no doubt that the man working in the store didn't hold a candle to Jeremy's tall, broad appearance, and it was a frustrating observation.

"What can I do for you, Jeremy?" he asked, his voice coming out with a tinge of something that sounded a whole lot like disappointment.

"I went to the bakery to look for Lucinda, and she wasn't there," Jeremy began, his voice gruff and annoyed. "So, I had to start looking for her, and I wound up here—with the two of you."

"Sorry to keep you waiting," Lucinda mumbled, embarrassment flooding her cheeks. "I'll see you..." she looked at the mercantile shop man, not recalling if he had given his name.

"Luke," he finished for her. "Luke Yutzy."

"Nice to meet you, Luke," she said, giving him a smile before turning around. She glanced up at Jeremy, who was looking past her to Luke. She rolled her eyes and trudged out of the store.

Jeremy might be loads more handsome than Luke, but at least Luke acknowledged her presence.

Chapter Seven

Does she like Luke Yutzy?

Jeremy's mind had been pondering the thought ever since he had picked Lucinda up from the mercantile shop a few days prior. He wasn't sure why it bothered him so much considering he had no interest in marrying her—though he still couldn't let it go.

I should be happy if she finds someone else.

If Lucinda found another man in the community to be with, it would eliminate his mother's relentless match-making.

And Jeremy would be free to focus on his leather-working business.

His father had always used the tack shop for mostly repairs, like mending broken bridles or occasionally crafting new breechings for the farmers in the community. It made for a great side business and was perfect for the season after harvest passed. However, Jeremy loved working in the shop—much more than he liked farming. He would be more than happy to give up farming and just work with leather.

I could hire someone to farm the land, while I just work in the shop.

He smiled at the thought and added it to his list of things to pray about. The list seemed to be getting longer and longer as time went by. Honestly, he felt a little stuck where he was, and longed for a change. Jeremy stared at the leather pattern in front of him, pursing his lips as he gazed down the outlining of a bag—well, purse. He was considering offering them for Christmas. The *Englischers* always loved Amish-crafted things, and he knew that the bags would be popular.

Maybe I should talk to the Yutzy's and see if they would sell some in their mercantile shop.

His eyes shifted to a couple bags he had already made, and Jeremy decided the following day he would take them to the shop. There was no harm in asking if they would be interested in placing them in their store. The worst thing they could do was tell him they weren't interested in them. The door of the workshop opening caught his attention, and he looked up to see Lucinda stepping through the door with a tray. A hint of beef stew wafted toward him, and he took a deep breath, enjoying the delicious scent of herbs and spices. That was one thing he couldn't deny about Lucinda—she was a good cook.

She also made stunning quilts, but he would never tell her that.

"Here's your lunch," she said, setting the tray down on the clear side of the work bench. "Your *mamm* wanted me to bring it to you."

"She always makes you bring me my lunch," Jeremy said, meeting Lucinda's eyes for just a split second. Lucinda pursed her lips at the comment and wandered away from him, heading for the shelves of leather material, tools, and patterns. It wasn't uncommon for Lucinda to stay around in the shop during the entire time he ate his lunch, though she never said a word to him. She hummed to herself and walked about, feeling the material.

Part of him thought she was doing it to try and see if he would strike up a conversation, but the more she came into the workshop, the more he realized that couldn't be true. No matter how little he said, she stayed, day after day. It was the most perplexing thing. He watched her casually meander around, her fingertips brushing the soft leather. Her dark blue dress fit her frame just right, and the more he watched her, the more he felt something stirring in his chest.

He bit the inside of his cheek, thinking of Luke Yutzy again. "Do you go to the mercantile shop often?" Jeremy asked, his own question surprising him as it left his mouth.

I need to get my tongue under control.

She turned to him, raising her eyebrows in surprise. "*Nee,* I don't. I've only been there just the one time."

"Only once?" he questioned, wincing at how gruff his voice sounded. There wasn't anything wrong with Lucinda going to the shop. There wasn't even anything wrong if she wanted to court a man from town. Luke Yutzy was a fine young man. In fact, he was going to be taking over the mercantile store, and it was a very successful business.

"I guess I just wanted to see what was in the store," Lucinda finally answered, shrugging at him. "I haven't been many places in town. I could use some more fabric, too. I'd like to make a new quilt for my bed."

Jeremy studied her face, not sure that he actually believed what she was saying. There was something off about the way the dimple in her cheek deepened.

"If you want to court someone in town, you know that's perfectly acceptable," he said, his eyes dropping back to the pattern in front of him.

Lucinda let out a heavy sigh, causing Jeremy to look back up at her. "I went to the mercantile shop to see if they were hiring," she said, her expression turning to a frown. "I don't want to be a burden around here."

"You're not a burden," he replied, furrowing his brow at the strange concern. "From everything I heard, you were forced to come here."

"Well, I *was*." Lucinda laughed softly. "I guess I just...You know the reason that I was brought here and well..." her voice trailed off as she looked back to the purses. "I don't know."

Jeremy shifted uncomfortably in his chair. He and Lucinda hadn't once discussed the reason she was at the house. In fact, they never really discussed anything. The conversation taking place right then was the most in-depth talking they had done since she had arrived.

"These bags are beautiful," Lucinda commented at the awkward silence growing between them. "I've admired them every time I come in here. I love the designs you tooled on this one," she pointed to one that was soft skinned leather, other than a central patch of hand tooled leather. It was one of his floral designs, though it was roses. He had even taken the time to paint them a deep shade of red, making the patch stand out against the black leather. Jeremy was especially proud of that one.

"Do you trace them on there?" she asked, turning to gaze at him.

"Sometimes I do," he said with a nod. "But that one was free-handed. Sometimes free handing designs work out for me—and sometimes they don't." He chuckled, reaching into a drawer to pull out the first attempt at the roses on another patch of leather. He held it out to her.

Eyeing him cautiously, she took the patch from him, her fingers brushing his ever so slightly. His arms were covered with goosebumps at the moment of contact between the two of them. The jolt of excitement that went along with it was just as startling, and he brought his attention back to the pattern in front of him.

"This is still very *gut*," Lucinda commented, her voice sounding like she might be impressed by him. The thought made his cheeks flush with a little bit of heat. "You're a wonderful artist, Jeremy." She beamed, handing the small patch of leather back to him. "*Gott* has really gifted you with something unique. I might be able to quilt, but to freehand something like that is, well, quite special."

Jeremy smiled, touched deeply by the compliment. "Thank you, Lucinda."

Her eyes lit up at his gratitude and she took a step toward him, peeking over at the pattern.

"Are you making another purse?" she asked, looking at the penciled lines before meeting his gaze.

"I was thinking of it," he admitted, holding her gaze for a few short moments. He hadn't ever looked that long into her pale blue eyes, but as he allowed himself to, his stomach flipped. They were stunning, and the softness in them drew him.

He cleared his throat and averted his eyes from her. "But I'm never going to get it done if I sit around and chit chat all day."

"Of course," she mumbled before ducking away and heading back toward the door. "I'm sorry for bothering you, Jeremy."

"You're not—"

The door shut behind her before he could tell her she wasn't bothering him. In fact, he had been enjoying the conversation much more than he wanted to admit.

Which was exactly why he had cut it short.

He was feeling a whole array of new emotions, and the fact that they were leaning in the direction that his mother wanted them to go, made him second guess his stance.

What if Mamm is right? What if she is *the woman for me?*

Chapter Eight

Lucinda couldn't get the small conversation out of her head, and how natural it had come between the two of them. She also couldn't stop thinking about the inquiry he had made in regard to her trip to the mercantile shop.

Is he worried that I might want to court someone else?

He had said it was perfectly acceptable if she wanted to court someone outside of the house. Why would he say that if he was interested in her?

Ugh.

She went back to sweeping up in the workshop, having taken on the chore while Jeremy was out running errands. She didn't want him to think she was just poking around in there because he was present. In fact, that wasn't the reason she ever stayed in the workshop, anyway. It was the deep smells of leather and paints that drew her. Not to mention, the different materials all felt so unique beneath her fingers. She often thought up beautiful designs that Jeremy could craft.

But she could never tell him of the things she thought of. Not because she didn't think he would listen, but because she wasn't sure she'd ever have the nerve to talk to him about it. He had been friendly with her the day before, but that was the first time he'd been anything other than aloof and distant.

And even still, he had quickly shut the conversation down without any warning. Jeremy was confusing—dashingly handsome, but confusing and hard to read. She continued to sweep the floor in quick swipes, moving the dirt, dust, and scraps into a central pile. Lucinda had never bothered to tidy up Jeremy's shop for him, but the last few times she had entered it, she had noticed it was in desperate need of a clean-up.

Maybe he'll notice and thank me.

She had openly complimented him, but he'd hardly said anything in return to her—not that she expected him to.

Especially after he had told her it was fine for her to court someone else.

Lucinda let out a frustrated sigh, not even sure why the mention even bothered her. After all, she had already told herself it was fine for her to court someone else. Just like she had wanted to find a job so she could eventually leave the Schrock farm and not be such a burden to the family. There was no use in her staying if she wasn't going to marry Jeremy. She helped Doris out around the house, but it wasn't like the woman couldn't handle things without her.

No one actually needs me here.

She paused her sweeping, reminding herself that she needed to write her mother back. She and Ruth had been writing Lucinda just as much as they had promised they would, but Lucinda wasn't doing a great job at returning the favor. Both of them often asked questions about Jeremy, but Lucinda never had anything to say about the man. She had to avoid the subject in nearly every single letter. She tried to focus more on the things they wrote to her about—like how her *mammi* was doing a little better or Isaac proposing marriage to Ruth.

And of course, Ruth had accepted the proposal.

It was clear her best friend was head over heels for Isaac, and she didn't blame her for being so. From everything Ruth had written, Isaac doted on her like she was the most wonderful woman in the entire world. It made Lucinda jealous, and she had to repent about it multiple times over the last week.

Just as she was dumping the pile into the trash can, the door swung open and in walked Jeremy, a huge grin on his face. She braced for his smile to fade and for him to question her as to why she was in his shop, but he didn't respond that way at all. In fact, his words startled her.

"You'll never believe what happened," he said to her, beaming. "I took the few handbags that I had made to the mercantile shop and there was an *Englischer* there who owns a clothing store in town. She made a *huge* order of them for Christmas for her store." The enthusiasm in his voice was moving, and Lucinda couldn't help but join in his excitement.

"That's so wonderful," she said. "Congratulations, Jeremy."

"Thank you," he continued, the light in his deep brown eyes meeting hers with an intensity that made her blush. "If I could have orders like this every year, I'd be able to hire someone to run the farm while I worked leather full time. What a life that'd be."

Lucinda was touched by the dreamy look on his face as he talked about it. "I would be so happy for you," she said, pulling the broom to her chest. "Have you made your own maker's stamp yet? You'd have to have something unique so that everyone would know it was you behind them."

"I have the one my father made, and sometimes I put my initials," he replied thoughtfully. "But that's a *gut* idea, Lucinda. I need to make an official stamp for myself. Maybe I could become busy enough that I would need to hire an apprentice, too. Wouldn't that just be wonderful *gut?*" He continued to rant with excitement, shaking his head. His grin was as wide as his face, and Lucinda was drawn to the way he was talking—and also worried.

I might be falling for him.

Her chest squeezed as she reminded herself of the way he had told her it was fine for her to court someone else. It wouldn't be good for her to fall for Jeremy. It would only lead to heartbreak.

"I've been thinking up some designs," he continued, rubbing his hands together. "I don't have enough leather here to complete the entire order, so I'll have to get an order placed with the supplier. The woman told me to make whatever it was that I liked, just because she knew they would sell without any problem at all."

"That's so exciting." Lucinda smiled up at him, her heart fluttering at his handsome dark features, and the way his eyes wrinkled in the corners when he grinned. She had never seen his expression so joyful, and she found it downright alluring. It was as if his demeanor was finally equaling out to his looks.

"Did you clean up in here?" he asked suddenly, his gaze shifting about the room and floor. "It's much tidier than what it was."

"I did," Lucinda admitted, nervously meeting his eyes. "I hope that's all right. I just thought you might want a cleaner workspace."

"Well," he said with a big grin, "I sure do appreciate that—I was just thinking I needed to do some straightening up out here before I got started on the order. Now, I don't have to worry about it. Thank you, Lucinda."

"You're welcome," she said, before taking a step toward the door. "I don't want to keep you from getting started on your order. I should go ahead and get back to the kitchen. It's my turn to make supper this evening. Doris is going over to the Millers for supper with Evelyn since her husband passed a few weeks ago."

"Of course," he said, his excitement suddenly fading a little. "I understand. I, uh, probably won't be up for supper. I have a lot of work that I need to get done down here in preparation for the order. I don't have enough designs, so I need to work on that."

Lucinda nodded. "I'll bring your supper to you later." With that, she headed out of the workshop and back to the farmhouse. She took some deep breaths as she made it back to the kitchen, surprised at herself for reacting so strangely to the conversation she'd had with Jeremy. In truth, the idea that her mother might be right about him—and that she herself might fall for him, was frustrating.

She didn't want her mother to be right—mostly because of the fight she had put up against her. It would be a little embarrassing to admit that all along the two giddy women had been correct about the match. Lucinda pushed the thought away and got busy making some bread for supper that evening, letting her mind wander back to the big order for Jeremy. He had said he didn't have enough designs for the order.

And she had more than she could list out, her mind running wild with different looks and patterns he could make. She wished more than anything that she and Jeremy could at least be friends. Lucinda would love to be a part of his process, and watching him cut, tool, and sew the purses would be exciting. It wasn't all that different from sewing a quilt, though she was certain it took much more artistic skill to conjure up such a beautiful bag from nothing.

Jeremy's gift was so unique and special. Lucinda decided she could at least pray for him in his endeavor. If she didn't have the nerve to discuss her ideas for designs, she could pray that *Gott* would guide him and make him successful in everything he did.

Chapter Nine

By Thanksgiving... I have to have the orders by Thanksgiving.

Jeremy could hardly take a full breath as he walked toward the house from the barn. He'd just gotten the order the day before, and when he had gone back to the mercantile store to put in an order for the leather, Luke had slammed him with the woman's deadline. He had agreed, mostly because he wanted the business more than anything else.

I'll just have to work day and night.

He grimaced at the thought. It wasn't that he minded working around the clock. Working came as natural to him as breathing. It was the fact that he wasn't sure even then if he could complete it in time. It was going to be a risk—and he didn't know any other leatherworkers in the area.

Pushing in the front door, he stepped inside the house. The pleasant scent of apple pie filled his nostrils, and he knew immediately that it was Lucinda baking it. Her pies had a heavier tinge of cinnamon. He'd never tell his mother, but he favored Lucinda's over hers.

"Is everything all right, Jeremy?" his mother asked, her brows furrowed as he stepped into the kitchen. "You look a bit stressed."

"That's because I am a little stressed," he admitted, shaking his head. He noticed Lucinda was standing in the corner of the kitchen but avoided meeting her gaze. Over the last few days, he had dropped his guard with her, and while that was seemingly all right ... he didn't want to make a habit of it.

The more he talked with her, the more he thought about her —and he needed to stop doing both. Thankfully though, the order he was going to be working on day and night would suffice as the perfect distraction.

"Are you going to tell us why you're stressed, Jeremy?" his mother asked when he had failed to elaborate any further on the matter.

"They need the order of handbags by Thanksgiving," he answered, not offering too much other information.

"Why on earth do they need it so soon? That's a month before Christmas," his mother exclaimed, her brow creasing with confusion. "They're asking for a lot from a one-man shop."

"Well, I suppose it has to do with the peak Christmas shopping time," Jeremy said with a shrug. "I don't know much about that sort of thing—I just know I'm going to get it done one way or another. I have to complete it on time if I want to keep getting orders like this."

"Do you need any help?" Lucinda finally spoke up, her facial expression looking just as hesitant as her voice sounded. "I would be more than happy to help you with anything that you might need."

Jeremy's jaw tightened, somewhat flattered by the offer, but also frustrated that he was in need of help.

"I think I'll be just fine," he snapped, inwardly cringing at how sharp his voice had come across. His mother raised an eyebrow at him, and for a moment he thought she might chide him for being so rude, but she didn't.

"Well, you better get along and get to work," she said instead. "Standing around and being cantankerous toward us isn't going to do you any good, I hope you know."

He winced at the jab. *I deserved that.*

Jeremy nodded to both of them and headed back out to the leather-working shop, not seeing any point in trying to make any more conversation. However, as he sat down at the bench to get started, he heard the door open behind him.

And in walked his mother, arms folded across her chest. "Now Jeremy Schrock," she began, her voice coming out in a warning. "Why on earth are you being so rude to Lucinda? That's how you've been to her since she arrived, and I just don't see why you keep after her like that."

"I didn't mean to be sharp with her, *Mamm*," he grunted, shaking his head. "I'm just worried about getting all of this done on time. If I can't get the order done, then there's no way that I'll ever be able to make a full-time business out of this."

"Well, you know *Gott* isn't going to favor someone who speaks so sharply to his future wife," she chided him, giving him a knowing look. "I'm tired of this kind of behavior from you."

"I'm not a child anymore," Jeremy said, doing his best to keep an even tone—though his annoyance was much more obvious than he would've liked. "You're the one who brought her here and expected me to ask her to marry me the day she walked in."

"I never said I expected you to do anything of the sort," she shot back, her voice growing in sharpness—there was no doubt she had been the one Jeremy had inherited his tone from. "Marge and I spent a lot of time in prayer about the two of you, and we're confident it was the right thing to do. You're being a stubborn, hard-headed man about it."

"Well, maybe you're trying to twist what you want into being *Gott's* Will," Jeremy nearly shouted, his irritation shifting to anger as he plopped down on the stool.

His mother's eyes widened, but she held her tongue, only shaking her head at him. She spun on her heel, exiting the shop faster than she had come in. The door shut loudly behind her, and Jeremy cringed. He hadn't had an argument with his mother in years, having avoided them by simply not speaking his mind.

I should've just kept my mouth shut.

"He's been working for nearly three days straight," Lucinda said quietly to Doris as she loaded up the bread and a bowl of stew onto the tray. "I'm not even sure if he ever sleeps."

Doris gave her a concerned look. "I'm not sure if he does or not, either," she agreed, letting out a sigh. "I just wish he would let us help him."

Lucinda pondered the situation for a moment, thinking of how dire things had gotten for Jeremy. He was in desperate need of help, though she was certain if either of them asked him, he would quickly decline their offers.

"There has to be something we can do," Doris said, her expression blank as she placed some silverware and a cloth napkin on the tray. "Maybe if we just go in there and talk to him, we could convince him—tell him how exhausted he looks."

"And we could offer to do something simple," Lucinda added. "Like cutting the material—or tracing the patterns. We don't have to do anything crucial."

Doris nodded. "Just the small things—things that he won't even think twice about us doing, but we'll be giving him some ample help."

"Exactly," Lucinda said, picking up the tray. She walked carefully toward the door, and Doris opened it for her so the two could slip out and head to the shop, where she was sure Jeremy was working. The two women had already taken on all of the evening and morning winter farm chores, allowing Jeremy to work through the night. He hadn't taken the time to tell them thank you, but he also had yet to emerge from the shop anyway.

Doris opened the door and gestured for Lucinda to precede her. "If he's too cantankerous, let's let him be for the evening, and we can come back in the morning."

Lucinda nodded, stepping into the workshop. No matter how many times she had visited it, the smell of leather was still easily just as surprising every time—in a good way. She loved the rich scent, and could spend all day soaking it in.

"How're things coming?" Doris asked Jeremy as Lucinda sat the tray down for him. Jeremy didn't look up from the sewing machine, steadily working the pedal-driven needle through the fabric. However, the dark circles beneath his eyes made it apparent that the man was downright exhausted.

"I'm not going to make the deadline," he finally said, his voice coming out strained and thick with defeat. "I don't see how I can do it. There's too much to do—even with the patterns already made and cut."

Lucinda studied the situation for a few moments, looking around the shop. It was piled with leather scraps and cuttings, and it was hard to tell which were supposed to be kept and which were supposed to be tossed—it was a complete mess. She also noticed the pallet of blankets in the floor, her heart squeezed with sympathy for Jeremy. It was admirable how hard the man worked, but it was awful how exhausted he was. However, before she thought about it too much, she saw a pile of patterns, laying on top of a stack of thin leather squares.

"Do those need to be traced and cut?" she asked Jeremy, noticing that he paused what he was doing to follow where she was pointing. A glimmer of hope sizzled in her chest as his eyes seemed to brighten.

"They do," he said carefully, looking up at her.

"How about Doris and I work together to cut those for you?" Lucinda offered, trying to sound as nonchalant as possible.

Jeremy hesitated, his gaze bouncing between his mother and Lucinda a couple of times. "I suppose that wouldn't be a bad idea—I-I could use the help."

Chapter Ten

"I'm afraid I'm going to have to get back to the kitchen." Jeremy's mother sighed, setting down her pattern. "If I don't, there won't be much to eat on Thanksgiving Day."

"That's fine," Jeremy muttered, his eyes focused on the small accent patch he was tooling in the moment. "Thank you for your help, *Mamm*."

"Of course," she murmured, pausing to squeeze his shoulder as she passed by him on her way to the door. Jeremy glanced over at her as she exited, letting out a sigh. There was no doubt that his mother and Lucinda had been much more help than he could've ever imagined. In fact, they were the reason he might actually get done in time.

Especially Lucinda.

She was detail oriented and paid close attention to every single instruction he gave her—even if it was a small task. She also worked with an enthusiasm that was admirable. It didn't matter how late she was in the shop, she always had a smile on her face, or was humming a lovely hymn. When she left, he found that it felt...*empty*.

"What if I stacked the squares of the cuts that need to be exactly the same?" Lucinda spoke up from where she was sitting across the room. "Don't you think that it would make the cutting go a little faster? I could use one of those blades instead of the scissors."

Jeremy hesitated, considering the idea. Every time Lucinda offered up some sort of suggestion he hadn't thought of, he was tempted to be resentful—but he knew it was wrong. There was no use in being overly prideful. Besides, Lucinda's ideas were nearly always good, and she had saved them a lot of time.

"All you can do is try it and see if it works," he muttered, trying not to meet her gaze. He knew she would have that giddy smile on her face, and it nearly always seemed to make his chest jump when he saw it.

It was annoying—and distracting.

Within just a few minutes, Lucinda was carrying an armful of pieces over to where he was working on stitching on the patch he had just finished.

"Oh, that's beautiful," Lucinda said, an awe to her voice. "I love that design."

Jeremy glanced up at her then, meeting her eyes. "Thank you," he managed to say, the light of the lamp casting a warm glow across her face. She was beautiful, and the more he worked with her, the more he thought so.

"Have you heard anything about the shipment that you ordered?" she asked, hustling back over to where she was cutting more pieces. "When is it supposed to be in?"

"Well..." Jeremy began, letting out a sigh. "It was supposed to be here today, but I would say tomorrow would be the most probable date at this point. Luke told me he would drop it by the moment it came in. He knows how bad I, er, *we* need it, so I don't think he'll hold off long once it comes in."

"That's quite nice of him to do such a thing. It'll save you a trip to town, so we can keep working on the bags," she remarked, her voice just as cheery as ever as she traced the pattern slowly onto the back of the leather.

"It is kind of him," Jeremy agreed, though his chest pinged a little with something that felt a whole lot like jealousy. Every time he went to the mercantile store now, he always ran into Luke. And every time he ran into Luke, Luke asked him about Lucinda. It was clearer than ever that the man had an interest in her, and it got right under his skin.

Which is exactly why he always told Luke that Lucinda wasn't looking to court right in that moment. But still, the man kept asking.

Jeremy swallowed hard, stealing a glance over at her. Lucinda had a stray lock of blonde hair that had slipped from her *kapp,* falling down into her face as she leaned over the material. She carefully cut the material, her hand steady and her eyes focused. His whole being wanted to stop everything and just admire her for a while, but he had grown to ignore that temptation. It wasn't appropriate for him to do such a thing— even if his mother was still set on the idea that they were to be married one day.

Lucinda rubbed her fatigued eyes, noticing that the clock said it was nearly one o'clock in the morning. She liked helping Jeremy out in the shop, but her entire body was too tired to keep going any further. She set down the knife she was using to cut out the pieces and dropped her shoulders for just a moment, letting the tension release from her neck and the top of her back.

She had been spending long days toiling away next to Jeremy, and it had caught up with her body. She had no idea how the man stood to work nearly all day and night without feeling stiff as a board. Jeremy was still sleeping in the shop, too. Lucinda had no doubt that he wouldn't be spending a night in his own bed until he was completely finished with the order.

Which wouldn't be long from then.

After all, Thanksgiving was just two days away. There was a stack of completed bags on one of the tables in the shop, and the stack was growing quite a bit every day. However, the more Doris had to spend in the kitchen preparing for Thanksgiving, the more Lucinda and Jeremy had to work by themselves, not having the chatty woman to keep the mood light. Lucinda did her best to keep it going, but Jeremy was never one to really want to converse.

She leaned forward, resting her elbows and forearms on the table in front of her. Her eyes felt extremely heavy, and she decided that for a just a moment, she would take a rest. She squeezed her eyes shut, and instant relief flooded her entire body, as if it had been waiting for her to do just that.

Leaning into the feeling, Lucinda felt herself dozing off, forgetting exactly where she was or what she was supposed to be doing. After all, what was just one little rest...

"Lucinda," a deep voice urged her in a hushed tone, and she felt a warm gentle hand on her shoulder, gently shaking her back and forth.

Her eyes fluttered open, surprised by the orange glow of the lamp. She sat upward, the realization hitting her that she was in the leather working shop still, and the nice warm hand was

Jeremy's. He was looking down at her with a deep concern on his face.

"You fell asleep," he said, his voice coming out surprisingly soft. "I think you ought to go up the house and get yourself some better rest. The shop isn't the place for you to be sleeping."

She blinked her eyes, still trying to adjust to the brightness—even though it wasn't really all that bright. "You sleep out here every night, Jeremy," she pointed out, her voice groggy with sleep and fatigue. "I just took a quick nap. I'm ready to keep working."

Jeremy shook his head at her. "I don't think that's a *gut* idea, Lucinda. You don't need to be out here working all night. It isn't your responsibility to finish all of this. I'd never ask that of you."

"I know that," Lucinda said, surprised a little by the way he was speaking to her. He wasn't being bossy or sharp, he just sounded...worried. "I don't want to leave you without help and have you miss the deadline."

"That's not going to happen." Jeremy chuckled. "I don't think you getting a few hours of sleep is going to mess up anything. You need the sleep. Otherwise, you might start cutting less than perfect lines," he added, a smile tugging at his lips.

The sight of it made Lucinda's heart jump. "Well, I suppose that would mean I was doing much more harm than good."

"Exactly." Jeremy laughed. "Why don't you let me walk you to the house? Just to make sure we don't find you snoozing in the yard when the sun rises."

Lucinda giggled. "Oh, what a sight that would be." She stood up from her chair, her whole body feeling stiff as she stretched her arms above her head and let out a heavy yawn. Maybe she was a lot more tired than she wanted to admit.

"Come on." Jeremy gestured, ushering her toward the door of the shop. As he opened the door, there was a strong gust of cold wind that blew through the door, and Lucinda instantly shivered. In the middle of the rush, she had forgotten to bring her coat with her that morning. Jeremy must've noticed her hesitation, because he shut the door, and turned, grabbing one of his own coats from the rack.

"Here," he murmured, offering it to Lucinda. "It's really chilly out there. It'll be a long walk without a coat."

Lucinda smiled, touched by the thoughtful gesture. "Thank you, Jeremy." She slid her arms into the sleeves, and he pulled it up onto her shoulders. A strong hint of leather and cedar hit her nose, and she breathed it in, comforted by the scent.

Jeremy opened the door for her again, and the two headed out across the cold, dark yard for the house. "The moon is quite bright tonight," he remarked as they walked.

"It's *very* bright," Lucinda agreed, admiring the way the beautiful light seemed to kiss everything around them. It even appeared to be glinting off Jeremy's face beneath his hat, and she found that his side profile, with his sturdy nose and long eyelashes, was made to look quite thoughtful when lit up by the moon. It was a sight to see, and she found that she liked it.

Quite a lot.

Jeremy paused for Lucinda to walk up the front steps of the house first, while he followed behind her. She had never noticed him do anything like that for her before, and she wondered if it was because she had earned his friendship working alongside him in the leather shop. Regardless, it was a nice change in how things had been between them.

She might even have to write and tell Ruth about it.

"Sleep well, Lucinda," Jeremy said, opening up the front door for her to slip inside. "I'm sure I'll see you bright and early in the morning."

"Oh, you most definitely will," she teased, laughing softly into the night. However, the more she giggled, the more she felt the fatigue washing over her.

And before she knew it, she was upstairs diving headfirst into bed, nearly falling asleep before she even hit the pillow.

Chapter Eleven

"Your leather order isn't in," Luke said with a sympathetic sigh. "I don't have a clue as to why it isn't here yet—I've never had an issue with such a thing, Jeremy. All I can come up with is the holiday is just putting off the shipments."

"Do you know if Mrs. Johnson is going to be in at any point today?" Jeremy asked, his chest tightening at the thought of having to tell her he might not make the order.

"She told me she was going to be coming in here around now, actually," Luke answered him, leaning against the counter at the store. "I am so sorry about the leather not coming in. Are you going to have enough to finish the bags? I know this is a real important endeavor for you."

"I don't know right now," Jeremy admitted, not wanting to disclose to Luke that he was almost certain there wouldn't be enough. Luke was clearly already feeling bad enough as it was. Jeremy didn't want to make him feel even worse when there was a good chance that the lack of material was going to ruin the entire thing. "I'll figure it out once I get back, but I ought to wait around and see if I can talk to her about the order."

"Maybe she'll let you run a day or two late," Luke suggested, giving him a somewhat reassuring smile. "I know she wants to have the bags for the peak holiday shopping right after Thanksgiving, but I don't see how a day would really make a huge difference—but then again, I'm no *Englischer.* You know they put way too much emphasis on holiday shopping."

"I've heard some crazy stories," Jeremy agreed, shaking his head. That was the one thing he had never liked when he was on *Rumspringa.* The world outside of their community spent way too much time worshipping things instead of worshipping *Gott.* It wasn't a good way to live, and he felt that it led to most of the problems they all had.

"Well, I hate to ask you this," Luke began, running a finger along the edge of the oak counter in the store. "But how is Lucinda? I know I ask you nearly every time you're in here— but I keep waiting for you to tell me she might come in here sometime and visit."

Jeremy's heart squeezed with guilt. Part of him wondered if he told Lucinda that Luke wanted her to visit him, if she would actually go to visit him. "I'll make another mention of it to her," he said, ignoring the part about how often Luke bugged him about it. In truth, he bugged him *way* more than he liked, and it was just plain annoying.

But admitting that would mean digging into the 'why' behind such a feeling.

"I can't believe she's been working alongside you in the leather shop," Luke continued, his voice coming out full of admiration. "That takes a right smart woman to learn so quickly. Rebekah said she's even staying up late to work with you. That's something special. I hope someday I can find a wife who cares enough about me to do such a thing."

Jeremy paused, never having thought about it like that—was that why Lucinda was helping him so much out in the shop? Because she cared about him? He hadn't ever thought about it in such a way. In fact, he only thought that she either sympathized with him, feeling sorry for the mess he was in, or that she was simply a kindhearted woman, who wanted to help. He actually leaned toward the latter, since Lucinda always went out of her way to help anyone.

Just like she was putting off sewing a new quilt for her bed so she could help him instead.

"Are you fond of her, Jeremy?" Luke suddenly blurted out, the question nearly knocking Jeremy right off his feet. "I don't mean to be so forward, I thought maybe *that* was why you always seemed bothered when I ask about her. If you're interested in courting her, you just have to say so and I won't ask about her—or show any interest in her when she comes into the store. You're my friend, Jeremy. I don't want to do that to you."

Jeremy didn't know what to say to Luke, and thankfully, the bells jingled as the door swung open, and he found himself relieved to see Mrs. Johnson, the woman who had placed the order with him. She was a middle-aged *Englisch* woman who reminded him a little bit of what some would call a cowgirl. She had dark, nearly black hair that was always braided beneath a cowboy hat, and she wore these strange jeans that were so large at the bottom, he couldn't see her shoes. It was a strange look, but he didn't pay much mind since after all, she *was* the one buying the purses from him.

"Well, it's good to see you here, Mr. Schrock," she greeted him, her voice warm as she smiled at both him and Luke. "I sure hope you have an update for me on the order. It's so hard to know what's going on when I can't just pick up the phone and call." She laughed, shaking her head. "I don't mean that in a bad way, of course. Your work is absolutely beautiful, and I'm certain your talent was honed because of the time and dedication you put into it—without the distraction of all our recent technology."

Jeremy nodded, not fully able to comprehend her ramble. "I guess so," he said, careful not to say anything that would concern her. He could feel the panic already rising in his chest as his predicament slammed back into him. "As far as an update goes on your order..." his voice trailed off, suddenly losing his confidence as she furrowed her brow at him.

"The shipment of leather that we ordered for him hasn't come in," Luke jumped in, sending a wave of relief through Jeremy. "I don't know why there's a hold-up on the material, but I'm sure it's got something to do with the holidays and what not. I'm hoping that we can get it in here either today or the day after Thanksgiving—I just can't be sure."

Mrs. Johnson let out a heavy sigh. "That won't work—I *have* to have the order in for my Black Friday sales. Would there be any way I could just pick it up Thanksgiving evening? That would give you as much time as possible to work while also still getting me a full order—I'm really counting on this order for my store. I've already advertised to the entire community. I'd hate to let them down. I always stick to my word."

Jeremy could see the concern on the woman's face. Her tone was kind and understanding, but she still drove the point home that she had people waiting on the order she had placed —which meant Jeremy *had* to come through one way or another.

"I'll have the order ready by Thanksgiving evening," Jeremy forced out the words, giving her a smile.

"So, if I come by your farm at around eight in the evening, the order will be ready to be picked up?" she asked, her eyes lighting up. "That would work perfectly for me if it does for you."

"I can make that happen," Jeremy said with a nod.

"Wonderful," she beamed, before bidding them goodbye and exiting the store. Then she looked at Luke. "Is my food order ready?"

"I'll get someone to load it in the car for you," Luke said with a smile.

She thanked him, nodded her farewell, and left the store. As soon as the door closed behind her, Jeremy let out a heavy sigh, running his hands over his face.

"You just made a promise that I sure hope you can keep," Luke said, shaking his head. "I don't think that leather order is going to be here in time, Jeremy."

"I guess I'll just have to figure something out then," he replied, his lack of confidence filling his voice.

Gott, please help me figure this out.

Chapter Twelve

Lucinda measured out a cup of flour and dumped it into the mixing bowl, careful not to spill much onto the counter. No matter how hard she had tried, she had always been a bit messy whenever she baked. It drove her mother absolutely crazy, but Doris didn't seem to mind. Probably because she, herself, was just as messy.

The kitchen and the rest of the house were full of rich holiday feast smells, and Lucinda loved the warmth and joy that went along with those. Some of the Schrock's relatives had already begun to arrive, and they had all greeted Lucinda in way that had made her feel like family. In fact, she found herself feeling right at home as she cooked alongside of Doris.

"I'm starving," Jeremy said as he stepped into the kitchen, the dark circles still present beneath his eyes as he rubbed the back of his neck. Despite his tall and broad stature, his fatigue caused his shoulders to sag more, and he appeared nearly an inch or so shorter than normal. Lucinda's heart squeezed at the sight, thankful that they were nearing the end of the tremendous order.

"How about you take some rolls back to the shop with you?" Doris suggested as she began to pile them up on a platter for him.

"Thank you, *Mamm*," he said, taking the plate from her. "I don't think that I'll be able to eat with everyone. Mrs. Johnson is supposed to be here at eight to pick up the orders, and I still have quite a ways to go—not to mention the leather never made it in."

"Well," Doris said with a sigh before turning to Lucinda. "I think it would be best if you went ahead and went out to help him finish up. There's plenty of free hands idling around that can help me finish up with the dinner, but there's no one else who's as much help as you are out in the shop."

Lucinda smiled, touched by the compliment. "If you don't mind, I think I will go out and help him—if you want me to," she added, looking up at Jeremy.

"Oh *jah*," he answered immediately, relief appearing on his face. "It would be much appreciated actually. I was sure hoping that you would be able to help me some today. You make things go much faster."

"Well then, let's go," she said, ushering Jeremy back out toward the shop. "All of the handbags are looking so lovely," Lucinda added as they headed back into the shop. She was going to miss the festivities and eating the large meal of Thanksgiving, but the thought of spending time with Jeremy seemed much better. She wasn't sure what it was about it, but she had grown to love working side by side with him—even if he did get a little grumpy when he was working.

Lucinda had opened the door for him since he was holding the platter of rolls, and they got right back to work. She started cutting the pieces for the final set of purses, while Jeremy worked diligently to sew up the few that were left. Instead of chatting back forth like they sometimes did, the shop was silent, neither of them humming or talking.

Occasionally, the laughter of the get-together at the house would waft over, and Lucinda would take just a moment to listen. Most of the time, it was children's laughter that she was hearing, and it warmed her to think about it. Despite not having been courted by anyone, she had always known she wanted a whole house full of children. The thought had always been one that brought her much joy and excitement, though it was often followed by a sad longing. She let out a sigh as she cut the final piece, using the very last of the leather in her pile.

Wait...

She paused, studying the pile of pieces and the list that she had made just to the side of it. Rereading her list, it appeared that she was short; she calculated quickly.

Three purses short.

Swallowing hard, she quickly recounted the pieces, hoping that maybe somehow in the middle of getting lost in her thoughts, she had just managed to forget to account for a few pieces. However, after checking and rechecking, it was apparent that they were short on material. Lucinda glanced over to Jeremy who was laser focused on his needle, slowly stitching up one of the bags.

It's going to ruin everything for him.

She shuffled through the pieces again, triple checking that the conclusion she had come to was indeed the right one—and it was. As she stood there silently, she waited for Jeremy to finish sewing up the purse. She knew that his reaction wasn't going to be a favorable one, and so she decided to let him finish, rather than stopping him right in the middle of it. She knew that might just cause him to slip and make a mistake.

And there was no way they could afford that.

Jeremy noticed Lucinda counting the pieces of material on her cutting table over and over again. His heart sank at the sight, catching the entire thing from the corner of his eye.

She didn't have to say anything to him for him to know exactly what was going on.

They were short on material, as he had known they would be.

His stomach clenched as he put the final stitch in one of the purses and pulled it away from the machine, cutting the thread with a pair of scissors. He set it down on the table and let out a sigh, trying his best not to panic at the defeat that was already creeping in.

"Jeremy..." Lucinda began, her voice coming out a little uneven and nervous. "I think—"

"We're out of material." He finished the thought for her, giving her a sad smile. "I had a bad feeling this was going to happen. I'm not sure what else we can do. I don't know if Mrs. Johnson will take an order that's three purses short or not."

Lucinda's expression made Jeremy's heart squeeze. "I'm just so sorry," she murmured, her eyes filling with a sympathy that moved him. "We would've finished in time, don't you think?"

"With your help, I definitely think that we would've come through just fine," he said, hoping to lift her spirits. Even though his own spirits were crushed, the sight of Lucinda being upset bothered him. He'd do anything to put the smile right back on her face. He didn't like seeing her this way.

She nodded, diverting her eyes away from his. "I guess I can just help you sew up what we have left," she said, wringing her hands in front of her. "Do you think that she'll order from you again after this?"

"I don't know," Jeremy shrugged, his shoulders sagging even more. "But I know that Luke tried his best to explain to her that we didn't get the shipment of material in time—and that it wasn't my fault. She kind of glazed right over that and asked if I could have them ready by this evening. I want to think that she will be understanding, but I really don't know."

"Well, we gave our very best effort, and *Gott* still sees it," Lucinda said, her voice lighting up just a fraction. "I think He would be proud of you for all your hard work, Jeremy."

Her words were touching, no one having ever said something like that to him. "I think He would be proud of you, too, Lucinda. You worked just as hard as I did—and you didn't have to. I know things have been a bit strained between us, but I can't tell you how much I appreciate—"

"Wait." Lucinda's eyes widened, her entire face lighting up. "I think I might have an idea." She spun around, rushing off to the bin of scraps, holding all of the leftover material that couldn't be used for the purses. There was quite a bit of it, though most of it was in strips that were very small and mostly useless. Jeremy had figured he would pick through them after the order was done, selecting what was good enough to be kept and what needed to be tossed in the trash.

"What're you doing?" he asked, as Lucida began to dig through it all, grabbing odds and ends. Once she had an armload, she rushed back to the table, laying out the pieces over one of the patterns. Slowly, Jeremy realized what she was doing—and just how ingenious it was. Within just minutes, she had the entire pattern complete, the strips creating a beautiful pattern.

"We can do it like this," she looked up at him, her eyes bright.

Excitement and relief swelled in his chest. "That's perfect." he exclaimed. Unable to hold back, he swooped her up by the waist, twirling her around. The surprise on her face slammed into him, and he nearly dropped her right back down to the ground. Embarrassment flooded his cheeks—he was completely mortified by what he had just done.

"I'm so sorry, Lucinda. That was—that was very inappropriate of me."

How could I be so brash with her? What is wrong with me? I should know better.

Chapter Thirteen

Lucinda felt breathless, staring up into Jeremy's dark eyes. "It's all right," she murmured, her heart racing excitedly in her chest. "I... I didn't mind it at all."

He held her gaze, his eyes locked with hers. "I guess, um..." his voice trailed off, just as the clock chimed. "We have to get back to work," he said, his voice rushed as he spun around and headed right back to the sewing machine.

Lucinda, taking a minute longer, also returned back to what she was doing. Thoughtfully, she pieced the strips together, ensuring that even though the handbags were made from scraps, they still appeared as though they were carefully planned out like all the others. It was a tedious task, one that took much longer than if she would've been working with new material. However, she did her best to stay focused.

I think I'm in love with Jeremy.

The thought was startling, but it didn't keep her from working just as diligently. If anything, she worked much harder than ever before, determined to make the deadline alongside Jeremy. She couldn't shake the way that he made her feel—and the fact that the two worked so well together as team. She was so immersed in her thoughts and work, she missed the sound of the workshop door opening, and Doris coming in.

"Well," she began, her voice startling Lucinda, "aren't you two just in here working like two bees in a hive. How're things coming?"

"We ran out of material, but Lucinda came up with the best idea," Jeremy said, his voice deep and excited. "She pulled the scraps from the bin and created the most beautiful pattern with them."

Lucinda's cheeks went red, and she looked down at her feet—but not before catching a curious look on Doris's face. "I did come up with an idea for the scraps," she said shyly, still touched by how proud Jeremy seemed to be of her.

"That's wonderful *gut*," Doris said, her voice full of awe. "Now isn't that something? I have to say, I'd never think that was just a bunch of scraps put together to make a purse. It's very artistic—I love the different patterns."

"Thank you." Lucinda beamed, glancing over at Jeremy, whose gaze was fixated right on her. She felt her ears begin to burn a little, and she couldn't help but wonder what Jeremy was thinking right at that moment. She hoped that even though he had apologized earlier, he hadn't regretted the moment they had shared.

The way his large hands had felt around her waist had given her the chills, and just thinking about it again, made it happen all over again. It was a wonderful, exciting feeling—better than anything else she had ever experienced.

And she wanted to know if Jeremy felt the same way.

Maybe he's in love with me, too.

She found herself hoping more than ever that the work would be finished quickly, and that maybe she would have a chance to speak with Jeremy about her feelings. At that moment, she wanted to explode with all her emotions, and share just how intensely she felt for him. She admired everything about him, and after working with him in the shop, she no longer felt intimidated by his cantankerous moods. He also didn't seem to be as sharp as he had been before.

"So can the two of you join us for supper? Or do you need to keep working?" Doris asked, her eyes bouncing between Lucinda and Jeremy. "It's all right if you need to keep working. I can always come out and bring a couple of plates for you. I'm sure everyone will understand. This is a big deal for your business."

"I think we should keep working," Jeremy said, meeting Lucinda's eyes. "At least, I have to keep working," he added quickly. "If Lucinda would like to quit for the night and eat supper with everyone, I don't blame her. It's not right of me to ask for her to stay out here and keep working. She already gave up the entire day to be out here with me."

"I'll stay," Lucinda said immediately, giving both Jeremy and Doris a smile. "I can't imagine not seeing this out to the end. Not to mention, I'm just as excited as you are." She turned to Jeremy, her cheeks blushing as they made eye contact again.

"Very well then," Doris said, clapping her hands together. "I'll go get the two of you some food and return. It might take me a few minutes. Is that all right or are the two of you starving?"

"We'll be fine," Lucinda said, already having leaned back over the table with the scraps. She was still working to use pins to lace the pieces together so that the sewing process would be easier and much faster for Jeremy. They only had about an hour before someone would be there to pick up the bags, and all she could think about now was making it to the finish line.

"Lucinda," Jeremy said softly, walking over to her from the table where he had been stitching. "I have to tell you something."

Her heart nearly jumped right out of her chest at the words, and she hoped that they were just what she had been thinking about him. "What is it?" she asked, the nerves apparent in her voice.

"Well…" His voice trailed off for a moment. "I think you should know that Luke Yutzy has been asking about you every time I go to the store."

Lucinda's heart sank—that was *not* what she was hoping Jeremy would want to talk about. In fact, she was hoping that he would want to talk about *him*. "What does he ask about me?" she forced out, trying to sound as nonchalant as possible.

"He wants to know if you'd be interested in courting him," Jeremy continued, his voice sounding strained as he spoke. Lucinda thought it might be the fact that he was so exhausted, but maybe…

Maybe he had feelings for her and *that* was why it sounded as though the words bothered him. After all, that day in the mercantile shop, Jeremy had seemed a little off when it came to Luke Yutzy showing an interest in her. Though, honestly, Jeremy had nothing to worry about when it came to Luke, because she only had her mind set on one man…

Him.

"But that's not really the part I need to tell you," Jeremy continued, his voice dropping off a little. "I think you should know that I've been telling him that you're not interested in courting right now. I know it was wrong of me, and that if you're mad at me for it, I completely understand. I just thought you should know the truth."

Before Lucinda could say anything to him about it, the door opened and in walked Doris, holding two full plates. There was plenty of food stacked up on them, including a delicious dessert. There was no doubt that she knew the state of hunger the two were in. After all, besides the roll that Lucinda had eaten at some point, she hadn't eaten anything else since breakfast.

"I wanted to make sure that you two had plenty to eat—you'd think those kin of ours hadn't had a meal in over a month with the way they're scarfing all the food down. It's amazing just how much food someone can put away on a holiday. I, myself, am a little guilty of it, but goodness." She shook her head, her voice full of pure amusement. "It's the young boys that just really surprise a body. I remember when Jeremy was young. He used to eat like that. It was like I had to cook for three additional people just to make enough food for him."

Lucinda giggled, shaking her head. "Just imagine when he has *kinner*. If he has a boy, I'm sure with his height, there'll be a mountain of food made to fill his belly."

Doris joined in on the laughter, though her amusement had changed to something a little deeper—joy, maybe? "I can't wait until the day that I have to make extra food for Jeremy's *kinner*. I don't think I'll ever complain about such a task. A home full of *kinner* is the perfect kind of home to have."

Lucinda glanced over at Jeremy, whose eyes were focused on the bag he was sewing up—one of those that were put together using he scraps. His cheeks were slightly red though, and she couldn't help but find amusement in the way he had reacted to such a statement. She was positive that only a few weeks before, he would've angrily grunted at such a statement.

But now he seemed to be just as caught up by the idea as she was. In fact, Lucinda found herself loving the idea of Jeremy having children...

Especially if they were hers, too.

"Well, I'll let the two of you get back to it." Doris chuckled as she backed toward the door to go. "I just thought that I would pass along the food, and I have to say, it's good to see the two of you acting so happy and joyful together. It's the perfect season for such a change, you know. I think the holidays are the most romantic of all the seasons."

Lucinda giggled as Doris left, and as soon as the door shut, she heard Jeremy let out an annoyed sigh.

"She's not so bad, you know," Lucinda pointed out, walking over the last of the bags for Jeremy to sew together. "In fact, I think she cares about you, and this is one way she shows it."

"Maybe so," Jeremy muttered, grabbing the last bag and beginning to stitch it up. Thankfully, it was a small endeavor and within just minutes of eight o'clock, he had completely finished it, setting the bag down on the table with a relieved grunt. "I can't believe we did it."

Chapter Fourteen

"Happy Thanksgiving," Mrs. Johnson said as she and a man who had been introduced as her husband met the two of them at the door of the shop. She surveyed the large order of bags, which Jeremy had assured her was complete. "I'm so thankful you had enough material to get all of the order done. I would've had no problem waiting for the remainder, given the predicament concerning the material, but I really appreciate all the extra hard work," she continued as her husband loaded up the purses. "I really think that these are going to be a huge hit with everyone."

"I hope they are," Jeremy said with a smile, standing closely beside Lucinda. "Thank you for your business and have yourself a wonderful Thanksgiving."

"You, too," Mrs. Johnson said, reaching out to shake his hand. "And your wife as well," she added with a warm smile.

Lucinda's cheeks went red, and she noticed that Jeremy didn't say anything to set her straight, letting the assumption go. As soon the Johnsons had left, they both collapsed into their work chairs, falling into silence for a few moments. Lucinda couldn't believe the rush of relief she felt now that the project was complete, and they no longer had to make purses all day long and all night. It was a fun, but exhausting feat—one that she hoped she didn't have to do again.

Not to that extent anyway.

"I hope she orders earlier next year." Jeremy groaned, running his hands over his face as he sat beside Lucinda. "I don't think I want to do this again—but thank you so much for your help. I couldn't have done it without you."

"I was more than happy to help," Lucinda said softly, reaching over to place a hand on Jeremy's forearm. The heat beneath his shirt warmed her hand and she took a deep breath, knowing exactly what she needed to do. "And to answer your question from earlier..." She paused as his gaze flickered to hers. "I have absolutely no interest in courting with Luke Yutzy. I already have my eyes on someone else."

Jeremy nodded, a grin slowly breaking out across his face. "I hear he's good with leather—is that the man you're fond of?"

Lucinda burst into a fit of chuckles, loving the side of Jeremy that had come out from behind his shell. "That's the one. He seems to just work day and night—he even sleeps in his shop."

"Well, he wouldn't sleep in his shop if he had a wife," he teased, shooting Lucinda a wink that made her stomach fill with butterflies. "But I heard he has his eyes on a beautiful blonde woman—she works just as hard and makes some of the best-looking quilts I've ever seen. She's a real catch. It seems like all the men in town have their eyes on her."

"Is that so?" Lucinda laughed, shaking her head at just how silly they sounded talking this way. "Are you hungry?" she asked her laugh fading a little as her stomach growled.

"Oh, I am famished." Jeremy sat up straighter, reaching across the table to pull their plates over to them.

"I think all of our food is cold now," Lucinda said with a sigh, using her fingers to feel the potatoes that were on the plate. They weren't ice cold, but they were definitely not warm any longer. All of the food had sat long enough that it had lost its heat.

Jeremy shrugged, picking up his fork. "It's just a little cool. It's still delicious Thanksgiving food—and I have a *lot* to be thankful for this year."

Lucinda laughed, grabbing her own fork. "I suppose you're right. What are you thankful for?" she asked, swept away by the look of affection in Jeremy's dark brown eyes. "You sound quite excited about it."

"Well," he began, clearing his throat. "I am thankful that *Gott* brought this opportunity into my life to start doing my dream business. I've always wanted to work leather full-time. It's been something I've wanted since I was just a *kinner*. I'm thankful for *gut* health and *gut* weather. But most of all," he hesitated, letting out a sharp exhale. "I think the thing I'm the most thankful for this year is the fact that you don't want to court Luke Yutzy."

Lucinda burst into laughter, shaking her head. "I think that might be the silliest thing I've ever heard someone say they're thankful for on Thanksgiving. It seems a bit off from what we're supposed to be thankful for."

"Hmm." Jeremy pretended to be put-off, a smirk growing on his face. "Well then, I guess the best way to say it is that I'm thankful for you, Lucinda. You make my whole life a lot better —and I didn't even realize it until we were stuck working side by side making purses. But you have to know, I'm sorry for how I treated you in the beginning—I just didn't want my *mamm* to be right."

"I'm thankful for you, too," Lucinda said, keeping her sentiment nice and short. There were more things than she could count when it came to what she was thankful for, but she knew the top one had to be the love she had developed for Jeremy—and the fact that he felt it, too.

The two said silent grace, before digging into their cold food. They both laughed together as they ate, sometimes making strange faces at each other as they tried their favorite foods in a whole new way. It was an evening Lucinda would never forget, as it signified the beginning of something she'd been waiting for nearly all her life.

However, as they finished up their plates, Jeremy sat down his fork for a moment, turning to Lucinda. "You know what this means, don't you, Lucinda?"

"What?" she asked, curiosity filling her face as she waited for him to answer.

"It means our *mamms* were right all along..."

She chuckled and shook her head. "*Jah*, you're right. But you know what? Right now, I'm awfully glad they were."

The End

Continue Reading...

Thank you for reading ***Mamm's Thanksgiving Plan!*** Are you wondering **what to read next?** Why not read ***The Wrong Path?* Here's a peek for you:**

The gravel crunched beneath Mary's feet as she trotted down the dirt road, nearly a mile from her quaint Amish home shared with her mother, father, and younger sister Susan—all of whom had called it night.

But hers was just getting started.

She picked up her pace, sweating beneath the thick green dress she and her mother had sewn two months before. Mary fanned herself as she jogged and sighed in relief as she rounded the corner to the end of the road. Amber and Denise were already waiting for her in their small pickup, flashing their high-beam lights as she approached. She wiped the sweat from her brow beneath her *kapp* and gave her *Englischer* friends a small wave.

"Hurry up, Mary," Amber called, leaning out the driver's side window. "We've been waiting for almost thirty minutes," she added, as the cool night breeze tussled her bleached hair.

"I'm so sorry," Mary said sheepishly, as she climbed into the backseat. "My *dat* was holding me up. I had to help with the garden."

Denise snickered in the front seat, her tanned knees pulled up to her chest. "You mean *dad*, right?"

"Right," Mary nodded, clicking her seatbelt in place, swallowing hard. "Dad." She had yet to fully catch on to a lot of the *Englischer* words, and despite her new friends' willingness to take her under their wing, they seemed to pick fun more than she'd like—but maybe she was just being sensitive. After all, the *Englischer* kids teased each other often, and no one seemed to take much offense.

"I heard there's gonna be a lot of boys at the party tonight," Denise said, spinning around to gaze at Mary, as she pushed a lock of stray dark-brown hair behind her ear. "Are you excited? You should let your hair down tonight."

"Mmm," Mary murmured, giving her a shy smile. "I'm not sure." She shrugged, trying to play off the nerves rattling her chest. Even though she had begun to socialize outside of the Amish community, she had yet to cross those lines—though she couldn't help but be curious. Amber and Denise wore a lot of make-up and always had perfectly styled hair, often paired with tight jeans and short tops that showed their stomachs.

Mamm would kill me if I wore something like that.

"Oh, come on," Denise pleaded, sticking out her bottom lip playfully. "Just one night—and I brought my make-up, too."

VISIT HERE To Read More!
https://www.ticahousepublishing.com/amish-miller.html

Thank you for Reading

If you **love Amish Romance**, <u>**Visit Here:**</u>

https://amish.subscribemenow.com/

to find out about all <u>**New Hannah Miller Amish Romance Releases!**</u> **We will let you know as soon as they become available!**

If you enjoyed ***Mamm's Thanksgiving Plan,*** would you kindly take a couple minutes to leave a positive review on Amazon? It only takes a moment, and positive reviews truly make a difference. I would be so grateful! Thank you!

Turn the page to discover more Hannah Miller Amish Romances just for you!

More Amish Romance from Hannah Miller

Visit HERE for Hannah Miller's Amish Romance

https://ticahousepublishing.com/amish-miller.html

About the Author

Hannah Miller has been writing Amish Romance for the past seven years. Long intrigued by the Amish way of life, Hannah has traveled the United States, visiting different Amish communities. She treasures her Amish friends and enjoys visiting with them. Hannah makes her home in Indiana, along with her husband, Robert. Together, they have three children and seven grandchildren. Hannah loves to ride bikes in the sunshine. And if it's warm enough for a picnic, you'll find her under the nearest tree!

www.ingramcontent.com/pod-product-compliance
Lightning Source LLC
Chambersburg PA
CBHW071335140726
47996CB00005B/1990

will never forget it."

Marissa took out her phone and snapped a picture of him. "We will call this the before picture, and then we will take one on the way home and call that the after picture."

"Are you expecting the two of them to be different?"

Marissa shrugged her shoulders. "I guess we will see on the way back now won't we?"

The rest of the cab ride to the hotel was relatively quiet and uneventful, however as they were driving past the beach Marissa saw a sign that said clothing optional and she couldn't help but smile to herself.

"Don't you think that looks like a rather nice beach down there," Marissa said pointing out the window as Ethan looked out the window with her.

"Yeah they don't have beaches like that in New York, that's for sure. I mean we can go down to beaches in New York but we don't have a tropical environment like this, with palm trees and beautiful sun and sand and, wow."

"Yeah I noticed the naked people on the beach too; I didn't think we would be able to see them from here!" Marissa shouted. "I guess they don't have to worry about any tan lines. Maybe we should check that beach out; it's not that far from where our cabin is situated."

As she made the suggestion she couldn't help but look at Ethan blushing again and smile. She knew that she would never get him to go to a nude beach, and she certainly wouldn't get him undressed at a nude beach, but she figured a girl can dream can't she? At least they would have a nice cabin to themselves, and hopefully he would open up and be a little less uptight when they were in private. She was hoping that the tropical environment would hopefully inspire them.

As they arrived at their cabin and got their bags out of the cab they could see that there was a nice board walk along the beach and they saw people drawing caricatures.

"Hey it's all those portrait drawers, why don't we go and get some crazy portraits made of ourselves," Marissa said. "It would make a nice souvenir of our first activity here in Hawaii."

"But isn't that kind of silly though, those characters always make people look crazy, I mean who goes around with a giant head rolling around on rollerblades?"

"But that's the point Ethan, the whole point of caricatures is that they're supposed to be overblown and over-the-top, they're supposed to be silly and entertaining like that, showing you what you would look like in an unrealistic situation."

"Well if that's really what you would like to do, okay then let's go get some crazy caricatures made."

They quickly got into their cabin and saw that it was small but was rather nice, nice and cozy and intimate. They quickly got dressed into clothing that was more appropriate to the climate, Ethan of course getting dressed in the bathroom, whereas Marissa didn't bother hiding herself as she just got undressed there in the bedroom. When Ethan came out and saw her getting undressed he put his hand over his eyes and apologized, but she said that she didn't mind him looking, in fact she would wish that he would look even more.

"Honestly Ethan sometimes you are too much of a gentleman, but it's nice to see that you are finally out of that winter coat now that we are in Hawaii!" She said. "When you are in a tropical paradise it's not inappropriate to show a little bit of skin now and again."

They went outside and they went down to the Boardwalk where the guy who drew caricatures started going to work on them. He drew a picture of Marissa with a giant head on rollerblades wearing a Hawaiian lei with her eyes bugging out of her skull.

"I think you look a lot prettier than you do in this picture," Ethan said as he paid for the portrait.

"What, are you saying that you wouldn't find me attractive if I had a giant head and was going around on rollerblades with my eyes bugging out of my skull?" Marissa said.

Ethan kissed her on the forehead. "No I would love you no matter what you look like, although I like the way you look in reality more than you do in some type of crazy caricature."

"Now it's your turn," she said as she sat him down in front of the painter. As Ethan sat down for his portrait she had sort of a wicked thought, she thought it would be cool if they painted a portrait of what he would look like naked, but she thought he would never go for that, and that would be kind of a weird thing to request for a Boardwalk painter.

At the end of the day the Boardwalk artist proved himself to be less than original when he drew a picture of Ethan with a giant head with his eyes bugging out of his skull on rollerblades.

"I guess getting a big head while you are rollerblading must be a popular pastime here in Hawaii," he said as he paid for the portrait and the two of them went back to the hotel to hang them up on the wall.

"I guess we can call ourselves the big headed rollerblading couple," Marissa said as they looked at the portraits on the wall.

"I've only been rollerblading once in my life, and let's just say it didn't go exactly spectacularly," Ethan said as he remembered that time he went rollerblading with his friends and almost suffered a concussion. It was the first time he went rollerblading and it was also the last time he would ever use rollerblades.

"I haven't been rollerblading that much myself, but again the whole idea is it's just supposed to be silly, the idea of everyone rollerblading with a big head is supposed to be funny," Marissa said.

"Well they are rather funny pictures; I will admit that, although even as big headed rollerbladers as we make a cute couple don't you think? So where do you want to go for dinner tonight? It will be nice to be eating something that wasn't an in-flight meal."

Marissa looked at her watch. "Well it's getting late, so we probably don't have time to do much else today, but I think that we can at least start off today with a good Hawaiian meal. Maybe we can even go to the luau afterwards."

The two of them went to a nice little restaurant that had all sorts of tropical dishes for them to try. They had a combination of seafood and all sorts of tropical fruit at a candlelit dinner.

"This is so romantic Ethan, I can't believe that I am actually going to be able to spend my Christmas vacation in a tropical paradise like this," Marissa said smiling. "I mean I like snow and everything, and always appreciated a white Christmas, but nothing can beat having a tropical holiday season."

As the two of them finished eating their dinner, Marissa had to admit that she was feeling rather amorous. Something about the warm atmosphere that she was unaccustomed to around this time of year was getting her all hot and bothered, and she was wondering if Ethan was feeling similar. Ethan may not have been running around naked on the beaches but she liked seeing him in short sleeves, shorts and sandals, even though he repeatedly mentioned how he felt rather silly about it.

"Want to go for a walk on the beach," Ethan said, as she was glad to see him showing some initiative. She actually thought that it was rather touching that he would ask that because they always joked about the fact that they met on an online dating service where both of them put that they liked long walks on the beach. They both put that because they had no idea what to put on a survey like that, and they joked that it was a sign that they were meant to be soulmates.

Marissa took him by the hand and the two of them started walking along the beach. The moon was bright in the sky, and it seemed like there was hardly any pollution, probably because Hawaii was so far from the mainland. They could see off in the distance was what looked like a volcano that they figured had been long dormant.

"I heard that they used to sacrifice virgins to volcanoes," Ethan said. "I wonder if that was really true or whether it was just a myth."

"Well I know that I am certainly in the clear on that one," Marissa said with a laugh. "But just to be sure we had better start doing it like animals just because we don't want to take a chance now do we?"

Ethan pulled her close to her and kissed her, and she suddenly started having fantasies of them stripping naked and having sex right there on the beach. They actually joked about that in their profile as well, they both seemed to think it was funny to say that their favorite drink was a sex on the beach, and she thought that it was funny that Ethan of all people put that in his profile when he was probably the last person in the world she could picture doing something like having sex on the beach, although she could still fantasize she figured.

As they continued walking along the beach at night Marissa had to admit that she had never done this with a guy before, and it was like her dream was actually coming true. So far they had only been in Hawaii for a couple of hours but everything was going exactly as she wanted it to. Ethan even seemed to be opening up a little bit and wasn't seeming as uptight, so she figured that maybe she had better take advantage of the situation while she could and get them back to their cabin on the beach.

When they walked into the cabin Marissa was about to start tearing her clothing off but then she had sort of a wickedly kinky idea that she had never tried before.

"That was a lovely evening wasn't it," Ethan said as he took off his sandals and looked out the window. "And we have a perfect view of the ocean and everything right here. I just hope that the sound of the ocean crashing against the shore doesn't keep us awake tonight."

"Well I didn't plan on doing that much sleeping tonight, if you catch my drift," Marissa said once again eager to tear off her clothing, but hoping that maybe Ethan would take a hint.

"I think I do," Ethan said as he started unbuttoning his shirt and very slowly taking it off. Marissa found that her heart was pounding just from that little bit, as Ethan really did take good care of himself. She figured that when you were paranoid and phobic about everything it paid to take good care of your health and to stay physically fit, another thing that she liked about him. He may have had lots of quirks but his quirks at least resulted in him having an attractive body.

As Ethan continued getting undressed Marissa simply stood there licking her lips and smiling. Although the lights were off, as they always were when they were about to be intimate, the moonlight was so bright that she could see Ethan rather clearly.

As Ethan stood there completely naked in front of her she could see that he was looking rather awkward and staring at her.

"So what exactly are you waiting for," Ethan said wondering why she hadn't taken off her clothing yet.

"Ethan this is going to sound strange, but I have kind of a weird little fantasy if you will indulge me."

"A weird little fantasy?" he raised his eyebrows, as now he was rather intrigued.

"Well normally I am the first one to get undressed and to just rip it off like some type of crazy person ripping off a straitjacket, but do you mind if I stay dressed for a little while and just admire the fact that you are naked?"

"Admire the fact that I am naked?"

"Yeah, just admire your body and everything like that, you have a nice one and you should show it off sometimes."

Ethan blushed and shrugged his shoulders. "I guess that

would be okay."

So as he stood there completely naked she started walking and circling around him like a vulture circling their prey. Ethan had to admit that this whole situation was feeling really weird to him, and he was wondering what type of angle that Marissa was getting at with this whole ordeal, but as she continued circling around him and smiling he had to admit that it felt kind of nice to be on display and to have somebody admiring him like that, even though he knew he was blushing profusely the entire time.

"Are you enjoying this?" Ethan said, looking awkwardly at Marissa and continuing to blush.

"You know Ethan I really am, it's sort of a weird thing but I just realized that I have never been fully dressed while you are completely naked."

"But you're going to get naked as well aren't you?" Ethan said, suddenly wondering what was taking her so long to take her clothes off, as this was a very unusual situation.

"Yeah I guess so," she said as she slowly started undressing and saw that Ethan was getting excited at the prospect. "Well I can see that you're certainly happy to see me like this, now you understand why I wanted to see you like this."

"But you have seen me like this plenty of times."

"Not while you were the only one naked."

"So have I satisfied your curiosity about that?"

She shrugged her shoulders "I guess so," she said, but she had to admit her curiosity was only growing and she felt weird about the whole thing. Now that they were both fully naked together somehow the buzz of the situation wasn't as intense.

Just the same they started going at it like animals, and by the time they were done Marissa had to admit that there was something about that brief little stretch of time where he was naked and she was not that made her feel exhilarated and got her in the mood like never before.

As she sat there lying naked in bed with Ethan and looking out the window at the moonlight shining upon their naked bodies, she had to admit this was one of the most romantic moments of her life, but at the same time she looked at Ethan there in bed and once again thought of her wish, her wish that when the morning came that he wouldn't get dressed again.

She shrugged her shoulders, shook her head and rolled over in bed with Ethan. It was unlikely, but the way she kept telling herself, a girl can dream can't she?

It was her first experience of being completely dressed while a man was completely naked and at her disposal, however briefly, but she was hoping with all her heart that it certainly would not be the last, and she looked forward to exploring this more in the future.

As she closed her eyes and went to sleep that night she couldn't help but dream of this being the new normal, however unlikely, but once again there was nothing wrong with dreaming.

3

December 25, Christmas Day.

Marissa slept rather restlessly that night because she was so hot and bothered by her night with Ethan that it was hard for her to concentrate on anything. The way she saw it she pretty much already got her Christmas gift by getting to keep her clothing on while Ethan was shy and naked in front of her, as something about seeing him all vulnerable like that and within her field of vision made her feel powerful like she had never felt before.

Marissa was always a very successful woman in real estate, and knew what it was like to feel powerful and successful, but she never knew what it was like to feel powerful and successful in the bedroom like that. She was always a little bit more dominant than Ethan, but the whole thing that had happened last night just put her over the top and made her feel powerfully in charge.

She couldn't help but fantasize about recapturing that feeling and was hoping that Ethan would indulge her further in the future; it was her Christmas wish after all. Christmas morning always made her feel like a kid again, at least until she realized that everything that she would ask Santa for would in no way be appropriate for children!

Marissa often felt like a pervert for all of the fantasies that she had, but she was a woman who owned her own sexuality and didn't let anybody make her feel guilty about it. In this relationship Ethan was the one who was a little bit more uptight, but he was never judgmental of her, and that was another thing that she liked about him.

As she yawned and thought to herself that she could probably use a little bit more sleep, she woke up smiling as she saw that Ethan was still naked in bed. Usually Ethan would get dressed right away after they had made love like that, but the fact that he was still in bed naked was just making her feel even more amorous, and she almost wanted to wake him up right then and there, but she was enjoying the fact that they were naked in bed together and that she could look under the covers and look at him as long as she wanted.

Once again she didn't really understand why Ethan was so shy, seeing as he had a really nice body, so it was a shame that he was always covering it up at the first opportunity. She was taking this opportunity to really revel in the fact that she was naked in bed with him.

Eventually however she got up and decided that she would take her shower but when she dried off she was eager to put her bathrobe on. Something about being covered up in her bathrobe suddenly made her feel like she had some little bit of power.

Slowly and carefully she walked back into the bedroom and removed the sheets from Ethan's body, so that she could watch him sitting there naked in bed while she was all nice and covered up. The fact that she was watching him naked in his sleep made her feel like a voyeur, and something about that got her heart racing at the thrill of it. The fact that she was looking at him naked and he didn't even know it was making her positively giddy, and she could barely contain her excitement.

As she walked around looking at Ethan's naked body she felt like tickling him, because she knew that he was excruciatingly ticklish, but then that would wake him up and end her fun. She couldn't help but point at his butt and laugh. Sometimes things like this made her feel really immature, especially for a grown woman, as this was more like something a teenage boy would do to a teenage girl that she wasn't suspecting, but she was just reveling in the fact that she was standing there fully dressed while her boyfriend was naked and out on display on the bed.

After a few minutes of watching Ethan she noticed that he seemed to be squirming around and looked like he was getting cold, goosebumps appearing on his body. He started tossing and turning as though he were trying to cover himself with the blanket, and she found it cute that even in his sleep he seemed like he was a little bit uncomfortable with his naked body being exposed like that.

Finally Ethan woke up and he saw Marissa standing there staring at him with a big smile on her face as he went to go cover himself up only to realize that she had pulled the sheets off of him.

"Merry Christmas my love," she said as Ethan smiled and blushed.

"Merry Christmas!" he said as he rubbed his eyes. "Hey, where did my clothing go?"

"I don't know, where did you leave it," Marissa said as she subtly pushed his clothing under the bed with her foot, not wanting this situation to be over anytime soon.

"I thought that I left it right at the side of the bed but I don't see it anywhere," Ethan said as he looked over the side of the bed.

Marissa shook her head. "Don't worry I'm sure it will show up eventually, weren't you going to take your shower anyway?"

"Well yes, I was, but I would like to know where my clothing is so that when I come out of the shower I can get dressed."

Marissa shook her head. "Why are you always so eager to get dressed in the morning, personally I think that your birthday suit is a good look on you!" She began laughing as she could see that once again he was blushing profusely and looking extremely uncomfortable. "Don't worry, you just take your shower and I will find your clothing for you, I mean where could it possibly have gone?"

Ethan reluctantly got up from the bed, and Marissa couldn't help but take a good look at his ass as he walked to the bathroom and started whistling at him as he turned around, looking extremely embarrassed, as she began laughing. She never got tired of teasing him like that.

As Ethan went into the bathroom to take a shower, Marissa knew that she should get looking for his clothing, but then she remembered she knew exactly where it was and she decided that she would indulge her voyeuristic inclinations a little bit more by very slowly going over to the bathroom door and peeking through the crack that was opening the door so that she could see Ethan taking a hot steamy shower.

Once again, although she was usually the first one to tear her clothing off, something about the fact that she was dressed and that she knew he was naked and didn't know where his clothing was was making her feel especially frisky. Wasn't she entitled to some holiday fun after all?

As Ethan came out of the shower and began drying himself off with a towel, Marissa couldn't help but resist the urge to open the door.

"Surprise!" she shouted, opening the door as Ethan covered himself up with the towel as she began laughing. "Sorry I couldn't resist!"

"Did you find my clothing?" Ethan said once again blushing and trying his best to hide it.

Marissa nodded. "But you're going to have to come out and get it." While Ethan was distracted Marissa leaned forward and grabbed the towel and pulled it away from him. "Yoink!"

"Hey come back here!" Ethan shouted as he ran out into the cabin as he saw Marissa standing there holding his towel wrapping it around her finger and laughing, and once again he was looking positively flush with embarrassment.

Marissa realized that she was being extremely immature but something about keeping his clothing from him and even just keeping the towel from him was making her feel a powerful rush of excitement that she didn't want to end. She didn't know why she was getting such an adrenaline rush from all of this, but something about it was making her feel powerfully in control in a way that she had never felt before.

"Keep away!" Marissa said as she held the towel in her hand before he came and took it away from her, disappointingly ending her fun.

"What has gotten into you?" he asked as he covered himself up with his towel before moving away from his body.

"What's wrong Ethan?"

"Well first off, you are acting like some type of horny teenage girl."

"Guilty as charged, you know that hole that somebody drilled in the girls locker room back in high school, that thing works both ways and I was very glad and thankful for that!" she said laughing and slapping her knees.

"The other thing though is that I seem to have gotten some type of a rash," Ethan said. "I feel like there is something wrong with this towel, like it's giving me some type of allergic reaction or something like that."

"So now you're allergic to a bathroom towel?" Marissa said shaking her head, wondering what he was going to be an allergic to next.

"Well anyway I guess I am dry enough, do you have my clothing," Ethan said as Marissa remembered it was under the bed. She figured that she had had her fun with him long enough and it was time for her to be nice and finally get his clothing.

Marissa reached under the bed and got his clothing and handed it to him as he slowly started getting dressed. However as soon as he was dressed he started looking extremely uncomfortable.

"What's the matter?" she asked, wondering what the problem was now.

She was shocked when all of the sudden Ethan suddenly started tearing off his clothing and throwing it to the floor and patting his naked skin as though he were on fire or something like that.

"Ethan I am glad that you decided to put on your more attractive suit," Marissa said with a smirk.

"But it's not funny, it felt like that clothing was burning my flesh," Ethan said as he continued patting his naked skin. Something about the way he was smacking his naked flesh like that was getting her excited again, but she felt that she should be serious for a moment, as something could actually be wrong.

"Burning your flesh? But you wear that stuff all the time; certainly you couldn't be allergic to whatever fabric is in your clothing just all of the sudden like that could you?"

"I don't know, but I could feel that my skin was burning, and I feel that it's producing some type of allergic reaction."

Marissa couldn't help but feel a thrill of excitement as he stood there naked and rubbing himself in front of her, it was once again giving her that great feeling of power that she had felt last night, but she realized that maybe she was being mean and ignoring what could be a really serious problem.

"Here, let me take a look at it," Marissa said as she began feeling his skin. She was genuinely concerned but that didn't mean she was going to turn down an opportunity to feel his naked body like that! She also smiled a bit when she could see him squirming around a bit because her touching him like that was clearly tickling him.

"Maybe if I put on a different outfit," Ethan said as he reached into his suitcase and began getting dressed. He stood there for a moment before he began tearing off his clothing and throwing it onto the floor just like the first time.

"No good?" Marissa asked now suddenly genuinely baffled at what was going on.

"I don't know what it is, but every time I put on an article of clothing it seems like it is burning my flesh."

"But I have never heard of an allergy that makes it feel like your flesh is burning just when clothing is touching it."

"Neither have I, and I have worn these outfits numerous times before and I never had any reaction in the past, it's just like I woke up suddenly this morning and it's like I can't even get dressed or something!"

That was when all of the sudden Marissa remembered her wish on the shooting star the night before, but that was a crazy idea, no way could something like that ever happen for real. She was open-minded about these types of things but that was just too absurd for her taste, and she knew that if she suggested the possibility that Ethan would say that she was being crazy, as he certainly did not believe in things like that.

"Well if you don't want to get dressed I certainly won't be disappointed," Marissa said laughing nervously but seeing that Ethan looked like he was genuinely concerned.

"But this is serious Marissa, let me try something else," Ethan said as he went through every outfit that he had but as soon as he put each one on he immediately started tearing it off and smacking his naked flesh, and it was kind of hard for Marissa to resist the urge to laugh, as she knew this was a serious situation, but she couldn't help but enjoy seeing him like that.

"It's not funny Marissa, this is a serious problem!" he shouted as he sat there naked on the bed covering himself up.

"I'm sorry, I realize this is serious, but it's kind of hard not to get a little bit turned on when you see a naked guy slapping himself like that. What do you think we should do? Do you think maybe I should bring you to the doctor?"

"I can't exactly go to the doctor like this!" he shouted, and she could see that now he was beginning to panic.

"Actually I heard that this particular resort and the whole

area is clothing optional, public nudity actually isn't illegal in the place where we happen to be, so you could actually leave the house like that and it wouldn't be a crime."

"Marissa I'm not going to the doctor completely naked like this, I'm not leaving this cabin like this, do you get me?"

Marissa nodded. "Yeah I suppose that would be kind of weird, and I know how you feel about going naked in public. Maybe we could get a doctor who makes a house call, I will just explain that you seem to be having an allergic reaction to your clothes and maybe they can come and see you here."

"Oh my God, this is just mortifying," Ethan said shaking his head and putting his face in his palms.

"Don't worry everything's going to be okay, here I'll call the doctor," Marissa said as she used her phone to look up the nearest doctor to see if they made house calls. She quickly made an appointment for the doctor to come see him right away and gave them the address. "Don't worry she'll be here really soon."

"She?" Ethan said already blushing, crossing his legs and rubbing his naked body with his arms.

"Oh God Ethan, don't be a baby, she's a doctor, she's really professional about these things, you know how many guys that she must have seen naked over the years? Hundreds, probably thousands! Hey maybe I should consider getting my PhD!" She could see that Ethan wasn't laughing, so she figured she had better stop teasing him. "I'm sorry Ethan, I didn't mean to tease you like that, this is a serious matter, but don't worry I am sure that the doctor will get it resolved."

Marissa sat down on the bed next to Ethan and there were several moments of awkward silence. Marissa figured that she had better get dressed before the doctor arrived, and that made her feel like she was really rubbing it in to Ethan, but she didn't really want the doctor to see her in her bathrobe.

Once Marissa was dressed she sat down next to Ethan and she could see that he was clearly uncomfortable, and once again she felt even more guilty now because she was getting sort of a power rush over the fact that she was fully dressed while he was sitting there naked next to her with no way to cover himself up.

Finally there was a knock at the door, and Marissa opened it only to find that it looked like it was Christmas carolers.

"We wish you a Merry Christmas, we wish you a Merry Christmas, we wish you a Merry Christmas and a happy new year," the carolers said until they caught an eyeful of Ethan sitting naked on the couch as he covered himself up and began screaming.

"Thank you for the lovely caroling, but we are actually waiting for a doctor right now, you see my boyfriend Ethan there is kind of allergic to clothing all of the sudden and –" Marissa started saying as Ethan kept making motions with his hand to close the door as well as putting his fingers over his lips, like don't broadcast it to the entire world. "Anyway thank you for the thought, but we really do have to be going."

"You could have given me a heads up before you opened the door like that!" Ethan said as he stood up looking defiant, but Marissa was finding it hard to take him seriously seeing as he was still completely naked and blushing profusely.

"Sorry I thought that it was the doctor!" Marissa said giggling. "But it was kind of funny to see the looks on their faces when they got a glance of you, and you should have seen your face!" But she could see that Ethan wasn't laughing. "Sorry, but it was kind of funny, you have to admit."

They waited a few more minutes and then they heard another knock at the door. Marissa made sure to look to see that it was the doctor before opening the door.

"I'm Dr. Spinelli," she said as she walked in. She was a tall and attractive woman, and for a moment Marissa almost felt jealous that she was going to get to see Ethan naked like that, but then she figured that she shouldn't be jealous of the doctor like that.

"Here's the patient," Marissa said, leading Dr. Spinelli over to Ethan who sat there on the bed cringing.

"Hi Doc," Ethan said, and they could both tell from his voice that this was excruciating for him.

"Well I guess I don't need to tell you to get undressed," Dr. Spinelli said as she laughed. "Sorry just a little bit of doctor humor."

Dr. Spinelli ordered Ethan to stand up and she started examining his skin and didn't see any signs of an allergic reaction. She then took blood, which almost made Ethan pass out, as he had a phobia of needles. Dr. Spinelli conducted a thorough examination of every inch of Ethan's body, with him sort of squirming around as Marissa could see that what she was doing was tickling him.

"My my, we really are sensitive to touch aren't we," Dr. Spinelli said with a smirk.

"Tell me about it," Marissa said with a big smile before giving a more serious look. "So what's wrong with him Doc?"

"Well I will have to see what the blood tests reveal when I get back to the laboratory and everything, but as far as I can tell from his examination there doesn't seem to be anything physically wrong with him."

"What are you saying Doc?" Ethan said. "It felt like my flesh was on fire when my clothing touched it."

Dr. Spinelli nodded. "You see here's the thing Ethan; don't you find it rather strange that the only thing that burned your flesh was your clothing? It seems like sitting on the couch or sitting on the bed doesn't seem to be producing any type of allergic reaction. And you say that you have not had any type of allergic reaction to these fabrics before?"

"Doc I am allergic to a very wide variety of things, but I have never had an allergic reaction to wearing these clothes before," Ethan said pointing to his clothing. "It's inexplicable; it really is just like I woke up this morning and suddenly I was allergic to clothing!"

Dr. Spinelli looked at his clothing carefully and shook her head. "But I have never heard of somebody inexplicably just suddenly becoming allergic to clothing, particularly all different forms of clothing that they had never been allergic to before. May I suggest the possibility that this is a psychosomatic reaction?"

"What, you're saying that I'm faking it," Ethan said. "Why would I do something like that?"

Dr. Spinelli shook her head. "Psychosomatic doesn't mean that you are faking it, it means that it's sort of in your head, that there is a psychological reason for why you are having this type of reaction. There is nothing that I can see that is physiologically wrong with you, but clearly this reaction is very real to you. I will have to wait until I hear the results of the blood test, but in the meantime I am thinking that maybe there is some type of psychological reason why you are having this reaction all of the sudden."

"Well we did take an airplane here, and as a result of watching that movie Snakes on a Plane Ethan was kind of afraid. And this is a new environment for us, as we have never been to a tropical place before. Do you think that maybe Ethan's fears of flying have made him break out in hives or something?"

"Like I said, there is nothing physiologically wrong with him, so he isn't breaking out in hives or anything like that, but I do think that the root cause of this problem could be psychological. I will get back to you with the blood test results, but in the meantime I would just try to relax and enjoy yourself. You said that you were here on vacation on the phone, and just be glad that you happen to be someplace warm and tropical, and also clothing optional."

"Thank you doctor, we eagerly await hearing from you, but don't worry I will take good care of Ethan in the meantime," Marissa said as Dr. Spinelli smiled and went towards the door. Marissa couldn't help but notice that she took one last look at Ethan and seemed like she was getting a good eye full of him.

"Well now what do we do now?" Ethan said as he sat there naked on the couch still blushing away hundred miles a second.

Marissa couldn't help but smile. "I say that we do what we came here to do, and have a very Merry Christmas!"

Although she had to admit that Ethan didn't look like he was as enthusiastic as she was, the prospect that he would be spending the entire Christmas day completely naked made her feel like she just got her Christmas gift already, and she knew that it was going to be a long and interesting day ahead of them, a Christmas that neither of them would ever forget.

4

"Come on Ethan, don't frown like that, sure it's sort of a weird situation, but we are still here in Hawaii having the tropical vacation of our lives, I think we can still have a very Merry Christmas," Marissa said as Ethan sat there on their bed rubbing his naked body.

"How am I supposed to have a Merry Christmas when I can't even put on any clothing?" Ethan said as he continued sitting there blushing profusely under Marissa's gaze.

"Well I know I'm certainly having a Merry Christmas," Marissa said giggling. "I'm sorry I didn't mean to make light of the situation, but I have to admit I'm kind of enjoying you sitting there naked, you really look just totally adorable."

He then began smiling before blushing again as he was clearly finding this whole experience to be extremely humiliating.

"The doctor said that it was psychosomatic," Ethan said as he shook his head. "That's a fancy way of saying that she thinks I am crazy."

"The doctor didn't say that you were crazy, she simply suggested that maybe the condition is psychological, maybe you are just somehow nervous over something, and if you stop being nervous about that maybe it will go away. What are you nervous about Ethan?"

"Well right now I'm nervous that I can't wear clothing!"

Marissa shook her head. "No, I mean what have you been nervous about leading up to this sudden allergic reaction, was it the fact that you were on an airplane earlier?"

"I thought that I dealt with the airplane pretty well, all things considered."

"You spent most of the airplane trip holding yourself because you were dying for a bathroom but didn't want to go to the bathroom any more than humanly possible, which I have to admit was just adorable as well."

"Hey it's not funny, it's a serious condition," Ethan said embarrassed over the fact that his girlfriend knew that he was extremely pee shy and couldn't go to the bathroom if anybody could hear him, including her, which is why she frequently would go to the bathroom door whenever she knew he had to pee really bad just to screw around with him.

"You know I think that maybe the doctor had a point Ethan, you really are a nervous and uptight guy, you know maybe if you weren't so nervous and uptight you wouldn't be having this allergic reaction. I think that we have to get to the root of what is making you nervous, and I don't just mean the fact that you feel nervous over the fact that you can't wear clothing right now, I mean I think that there is something that you are really stressing over that is perhaps making you break out in this allergic reaction, and we just have to figure out what it is."

Ethan had to admit that there was something that he was stressing over, something that he didn't want to admit to her because it would ruin the surprise, so for now he would have to keep it secret, although he didn't know if he would be able to keep it secret if it meant that he wouldn't be able to wear clothing. You don't exactly want to propose to your girlfriend completely buck naked like that, even though the way Marissa was smiling right now she would probably absolutely love that.

"You know it was probably just the airplane ride, you are right, I was probably afraid of the airplane because of, well you know, Snakes on a Plane and the Twilight Zone. But I am sure if I just relax I will be able to put on my clothing in no time."

"That's the spirit; just calm down and we will get some clothing on that naked ass!" Marissa said trying hard not to laugh but still enjoying the situation regardless. She felt a little bit mean over the fact that she was getting such a kick out of Ethan's condition, but she had to admit the prospect of a boyfriend who couldn't wear clothing was something that she would have a much easier time dealing with than he would.

For a moment she felt guilty again when she thought to the wish that she had made on the shooting star, until she shook her head and realized that that was completely insane. There is no way wishing on a shooting star was the reason why Ethan couldn't wear clothing, he didn't even know that she had wished on a star like that, so how could he be having a psychosomatic reaction to something that he didn't even know about?

"Maybe if I get some breakfast in me I will feel better," Ethan said. "You know that I'm really good at making pancakes."

"That sounds like a good idea, I am sure that once we have eaten something we will both be feeling a whole lot better, every situation looks better when you have a full stomach."

"Do you think you can just maybe do something for me and maybe give me a little bit of privacy? I'm self-conscious about cooking."

"Self-conscious about cooking, eh?" Marissa said raising an eyebrow knowing that it wasn't the cooking that he was self-conscious about, so much as the fact that he was completely buck naked. "Okay Ethan I will let you make breakfast, and maybe that will calm you down, and afterwards maybe you will be able to get dressed."

As Ethan went into the kitchen to begin cooking his famous Christmas morning pancake surprise, Marissa had to admit that this whole thing was getting really crazy. Was Ethan really never going to be able to wear clothing again? The prospect of course was exciting to her, but she realized how impractical that would be, so as much as she was enjoying that she was hoping that whatever was bothering Ethan that he would be able to get over it and get back to normal so that they could get on with enjoying their vacation.

As Marissa smelled the food coming from the kitchen, she had to admit she couldn't resist her curiosity. Although she said she would give Ethan privacy, the prospect of a guy cooking breakfast naked for her was exciting her like nothing else before. She always liked the idea of a man serving her breakfast naked, although she always felt too shy to tell Ethan about that, because she felt that it would probably make him feel uncomfortable. But now that he was just a few feet away in the other room completely buck naked making pancakes she could be forgiven for a little bit of perverted curiosity.

Very slowly she tiptoed over to just outside the kitchen where she could get a good view of Ethan flipping the pancakes, and for a moment it was like while he was cooking he had completely forgot about the fact that he was naked. He was sort of shaking his ass in a way that Marissa found completely intoxicating, and it took every amount of restraint not to get out her phone and begin recording him, but she knew that he would feel that to be a violation of his privacy, and she knew that he wouldn't go for that.

"Okay girl, try to control yourself," Marissa said but she couldn't take her eyes off of Ethan's ass which was going back and forth as he made the pancakes. Looking to make sure that nobody else was looking in her general direction, she found her hand slipping into her pants and she couldn't help but masturbate to this whole scene. This was like her fantasy come true, a naked man cooking her breakfast, it really was a Merry Christmas for her and the day had only just started!

"Pancakes are served," Ethan said as he stuck his head outside of the kitchen as Marissa pulled her hands out of her pants quickly and began whistling in a nonchalant manner so that Ethan wouldn't suspect that she had just been masturbating to his culinary delights.

"I'll be right there," Marissa said as she walked into the kitchen to see Ethan standing there, still blushing profusely, but completely naked. She couldn't help but have her eyes gravitate immediately towards his genitals. Pancakes, pancock was more like it!

As Marissa sat down at the breakfast table and Ethan put the pancakes onto her plate, she had to admit that she was practically swooning over the fact that a naked man was now serving her breakfast. The sexual tension that was being generated by this was driving her completely out of her mind, and it took every ounce of self-control she had not to put her hands immediately back in her pants.

She didn't know what it was, but something about a man doing domestic little duties for a woman like that while completely and utterly naked was making her feel like rush of power like she couldn't even begin to comprehend.

As the two of them sat down at the breakfast table and began pouring the syrup on their pancakes, Marissa couldn't help but think that this image brought to mind something else that she would like to be doing at that very moment. But she thought that she had to restrain herself for Ethan's sake and try to be nonchalant about everything that was going on.

As she sat across from Ethan, sitting naked not more than a couple of inches away, she started slowly eating her pancakes, savoring each sensuous bite as she couldn't help but notice that Ethan was smiling as well, even though he was still blushing like crazy.

Marissa had never eaten a meal across from a naked man before, but something about the fact that Ethan was naked was making her pancakes taste even better.

"These are really good Ethan, I mean really really good," Marissa said feeling as though she were about to have an orgasm just from the taste of the pancakes combined with the fact that she was eating them across from her naked boyfriend.

At that moment she thought to herself strangely the reason why this might be so exciting for her, she could never remember a time when Ethan had been naked in such an obvious way for such a prolonged amount of time, and she was eating up every moment of it just as quickly as she was eating up the pancakes.

"Really, you don't think that they are too sweet," Ethan said as he ate his pancakes.

"Oh this is really sweet Ethan, but that's a good thing," Marissa said and she wasn't exactly talking entirely about the pancakes.

They continued eating their breakfast, and Marissa couldn't

help but put one hand underneath the table and down her pants. She was hoping that maybe Ethan wouldn't notice, or maybe she was hoping that he would notice, as she started masturbating while finishing up the last of her pancakes.

"But I have to say you are looking rather satisfied with those pancakes," Ethan said, still blushing, and she could see that he was sensing the sexual tension in the room as well.

"Oh my God I am," Marissa said as she could feel herself orgasming while trying not to choke on her pancakes in the process.

"Well I guess I had better clear the table then," Ethan said as he started clearing their empty plates and putting them in the sink. As Marissa sat there continuing to masturbate as she watched Ethan's ass go up and down while he washed the dishes, she could contain herself no longer.

Very slowly she got up and put her hands on Ethan's ass and began running her fingernails up and causing him to jump up.

"Marissa you know I'm very ticklish, you know around there!" he shouted.

As he turned around and looked Marissa in the eye he could feel all the blood rushing into his genitals. He didn't know what it was about the situation, but he found this perhaps the most erotically charged moment of his life, and the next thing he knew Marissa was pushing him towards the bedroom.

"Those pancakes aren't going to be the only thing making us sticky this morning," she said as she pushed him down on the bed and dove on top of him like a rabid animal.

Christmas had barely even started, and already she could say that it was by far the most Merry Christmas she had ever remembered, and one that she would never forget.

5

The two of them laid in bed together for a long time, not exactly sure what to say about what had just happened. Maybe it was something that didn't need any articulation in words, but as the two of them laid there naked in bed together there was a feeling of satisfaction between the two of them, a sense of equality between the two of them, as though there were a natural balance of power that had been restored.

"You know it's been a long time since we had sex in the morning and everything like that, you didn't even turn out the lights," Marissa said with a big smile. "I'm pretty proud of you."

"What just happened," Ethan said smiling and looking satisfied.

Marissa smiled again. "Well what I think happened was my hot boyfriend made me breakfast completely naked and then I became uncontrollably horny and I took you into the bedroom and started having mad passionate love with you without even taking off my clothing right away, then one thing led to another and now it looks like we are both naked."

"Yeah that sounds pretty accurate," Ethan said as he laughed. "I don't know what it was but something about that whole situation, I guess I had never been in that situation before, but me making you breakfast like that completely naked, and you just watching me like some type of horny schoolgirl, I don't know it just it was like."

"It was the most fucking intense thing that I have ever experienced in my life!" she said as she put her arms behind her head underneath her pillow. "I mean my God Ethan that was the hottest thing ever. I felt kind of weird bringing it up but something about a man making me breakfast naked, it's always been kind of a fantasy of mine, and let's just say you've made this a very Merry Christmas for me that is for sure."

"You know I don't know what it was about the whole situation but I found it really hot as well. I don't know if it was just because I was naked or because I was making you breakfast or what, but something about it just felt, I don't know, I just really don't know how to describe it, I've never felt that before."

"You know what I think it was Ethan; I think that you are starting to learn to like the feeling of being naked."

"Hey we've made love plenty of times, I have nothing against naked."

"I know you Ethan, and although we have made love plenty of times we have never done it with the lights on before, you're the most bashful guy I know, and I love that about you, and I think maybe that's what made it so hot. I think the fact that me looking at you while you were completely naked like that; I think just the fact that it was making you crazy was what made it so satisfying when we finally made love."

"Wow, really, you think so?"

"Think about it Ethan, I can't remember you ever being naked like this for such a prolonged amount of time, and certainly not when I get to you, you know, keep everything on."

Ethan turned to her and looked her directly in the eye. "You know this is going to sound crazy but I can't help get the feeling that something about the fact that you got to keep it all on this time, were you getting off on that?"

Marissa could tell that he had somehow figured her out and she smiled. "Well Ethan, I suppose guilty as charged. I don't know what it was but, I don't know if it's just because it was something different, or something the reversal of the usual norm, but something about it just got me hotter than ever before. I mean normally I am the first one to strip out of my clothing and everything like that, but that feeling of getting to keep my clothing on while you were all naked and squirming around, all uncomfortable and embarrassed and blushing like a tomato like that, I just never felt such an intense and exciting feeling before. It's like all the blood started rushing down below. And you know what else Ethan?"

"What's that?"

"I think that you liked it, I think that you liked it a lot. Don't lie to me, you enjoyed that every bit as much as I did, maybe even more."

Ethan smiled and kissed her. "I guess I can't deny that, I mean not that I want to be allergic to clothing or anything like that, but something about this whole experience, I don't know, I've just never experienced it before and, I don't know, it was something different, and I can say that I liked it."

"I can't believe that I started fucking you before I even got undressed, now that's really unlike me! Usually I can't wait to rip out of my clothing, but something about the power rush that I was getting from getting to keep my clothing on while you were naked beneath me like my own personal plaything, my God Ethan it was like the hottest thing in the world!"

"Well it was certainly an experience, I'll say that much. But wait a minute, I just thought of something!"

"What are you talking about Ethan?"

"Your clothing!"

"What about my clothing, it's not on me right now, I'm sure

that you're happy about that!"

"No, I mean when you were on top of me wearing all of your clothing and everything like that, the fabric of your clothing was touching my skin and I wasn't having an allergic reaction!"

"Hey you are right, you didn't have an allergic reaction, and maybe your allergic reaction is over. Maybe all you had to do was overcome your uptightness about perhaps me seeing you naked while I was getting to stay dressed and that cured you of your condition. You're cured Ethan, now you can get dressed again, although I hope that maybe you will maybe wait a little while, know what I mean?"

Ethan smiled and kissed her as the two of them sat in bed together. There was something nice about lying naked in bed together when he knew that he would be able to put his clothing on once again when they got out of bed. That was immediately causing him to start to relax again, and after all of that lovemaking he was rather exhausted. Maybe that release was finally able to get him over his condition, maybe just needed to overcome his inhibitions and now everything was going to be okay after all.

Marissa eventually got out of bed, and Ethan couldn't help but stare at her ass as she did so. He always was an ass man, and she really did have the perfectly sculpted ass, like something you would see on one of those old Greek statues of a Greek goddess or something like that. That was an ass that you could set your watch by, well if he was wearing a watch, although right now he was still wearing nothing.

As he watched Marissa walk around the room naked, staring at her, he kind of understood what she felt when he was uncovered like that. There's something about seeing your lover walking around completely vulnerable and exposed like that, the feeling of trust that they have to do that around you, that gave him a really good feeling inside, and he kind of realized that he was silly for always being so shy around her all the time, and maybe it took an incident like this to show him that.

"I think that I am going to go take a shower because I feel a little bit dirty, and I think that I should get freshened up before our guests arrive," Marissa said as she winked at him and started walking towards the shower. As he watched her ass going up and down he took that as a cue that she was inviting him to join her.

As he got up from bed he paused for a moment as he remembered what she had just said. "Guests," he said shaking his head. He shrugged his shoulders; he figured it really didn't matter if they were going to be having guests as long as he was able to cover himself up.

He followed Marissa into the shower, and soon the two of them were underneath nice warm hot water, their naked bodies dripping wet together as they began making out in the steam of the shower. He couldn't believe that they had never done this before, and now he was thinking that he really was rather uptight. Who wouldn't want to take a shower naked with a beautiful woman like that?

As the two of them rubbed soapy suds all over their naked bodies and helped each other get to those hard to reach places, he had to admit that this was really nice. He was feeling really relaxed, and whatever stress or tension that he was feeling earlier was just leaving his body and being replaced with a pleasant feeling of blissfulness. There was something really relaxing about the hot water pouring against them, the two of them sitting there, or standing there rather, together naked with not a care in the world, the entire outside world going away.

When they were finished with their shower they got out of the shower together and began toweling each other off, drying themselves off, before standing there naked in front of the mirror together and smiling.

"We really do make a cute naked couple, almost makes you wonder what Adam and Eve looked like," Marissa said as he nodded in agreement. They actually did look rather nice together naked in the mirror like that, something about seeing their own naked reflections was interesting, he had never really stopped and looked at his naked reflection before like that, but standing there naked next to the woman of his dreams he had to admit that they looked just right together, clothing or no clothing.

Once they left the bathroom Marissa began throwing on her clothing and smiling. Ethan was about to reach for his clothing but he saw her standing there shaking her head and waving her finger, almost like some type of nanny telling a young child ah ah ah, it's not time to get dressed yet, so he simply complied and enjoyed the fact that they stood there naked holding each other in each other's arms, feeling her fingernails tracing their way down his naked flesh and causing him to get goosebumps.

"You know you really are the most ticklish guy I have ever been with," Marissa said. "Maybe you just have sensitive skin, maybe which was why you are having that allergic reaction before. At any rate I do like seeing your skin crawl and break out in goosebumps like that. And I like the fact that even after everything you are still freaking blushing!"

Ethan scrunched his face up. "I can't help it, there is something a little bit embarrassing about being the only one naked, it makes you feel even more naked, if that makes sense, know what I mean?"

Marissa nodded. "Yes there is something exciting about that isn't there? But you know I think I like the fact that you are shy about this, that's probably what made it so intense, watching you as a bunch of squirming flesh right there under my gaze, it's a powerful feeling, a powerful feeling that I don't think that a woman gets to experience as much as a man does. Men are used to looking at naked women but I don't think that naked men are used to being looked at by dressed women in the same way."

"But you know I had never thought about it like that, but I guess you are right, I have never felt so vulnerable and exposed like this before, and I think that it is sort of a weird feeling as a man, not a bad feeling mind you, just very very different."

"I like it, I like it a lot," she said as she kissed him.

"Well as much as you like it I suppose at some point of the day I'm going to have to get dressed, especially if you are expecting guests later."

Marissa nodded. "As much as I hate to admit it I suppose you are right, we have a bunch of things to do before the guests arrive, so I guess we had both better get dressed and get to it."

Ethan nodded and smiled as he went to his suitcase and started taking his clothing out and putting it on. As he stood there finally dressed again he once again felt comfortable in his own skin, although it was sort of a nice feeling to have experienced what it was like to be vulnerable in front of Marissa like that, but he felt a lot more secure now that he was once again wearing the pants.

However that was when he suddenly noticed something as he immediately began tearing off his clothing and smacking at his skin. When Marissa came back into the room she found him completely naked and was smiling.

"Well well well, at first you are shy about being naked, and now you can't bear to put your clothing back on," Marissa said laughing out loud.

"It's not that Marissa, I'm having the same reaction, as soon as I put my clothing back on it suddenly felt like my skin was on fire again!"

"But I thought that you cured yourself, I thought that getting over your inhibitions and all your uptightness helped you to feel comfortable in your own skin and let you put your clothing back on."

"I don't get it, when we were in bed together and you were dressed and were on top of me and your clothing was rubbing against my skin it didn't have the same effect."

Marissa suddenly laughed.

"What's so funny?" Ethan demanded. "I don't consider this to be a laughing matter!"

"Ethan this is going to sound crazy, and I swear it's not just so that I can indulge some type of weird perverted curiosity, but maybe it's something with your clothing specifically that is the problem."

"What exactly are you suggesting?"

Marissa started stripping out of her clothing as he then looked on with curiosity and horniness before she handed him her clothing.

"What do you want me to do with this?" Ethan said as he grabbed her clothing from her.

"Put it on, let's see if it has the same reaction."

"You mean you're serious?" Ethan said rolling his eyes. "And you really mean that this just isn't because you want to see what I look like in women's clothing?"

"No Ethan I swear, let's just see what happens."

Ethan took a moment to get changed, as Marissa couldn't help but watch in enjoyment, and in a moment Ethan was standing there wearing Marissa's clothing and looking absurd as she stood there naked. She had to admit that this didn't give her the same feeling as being fully dressed while Ethan was naked, but she also couldn't deny that there was something extremely entertaining and amusing about this and she couldn't help but laugh.

Ethan simply shook his head as he started pulling off

Marissa's clothing.

"Marissa I think that we have a majorly serious problem here," he said and that was when they both stopped laughing.

6

"I don't know what happened, I was fine just a few moments ago, how come I am experiencing the allergic reaction again, when just having your clothing rubbing against me wasn't doing anything," Ethan said.

Marissa shook her head. "I don't know Ethan, maybe it was because the clothing was just brushing up against you and wasn't like pressed tightly against your skin. I don't know, I've never seen a condition like this before. But just relax; I am sure that whatever it is that we can deal with it."

"We can deal with it, what do you have to deal with, you're not the one who is completely buck naked and has no possible way of covering yourself up!"

"Hey I'm dealing with this in my own way; I have to deal with the fact that my hot boyfriend is stuck completely naked. Okay when I say it like that it doesn't really sound all that bad, so I can see how you are probably coming at it from a different angle than me. But just because I am kind of enjoying the situation doesn't mean that I am not sympathetic to the situation. I realize that in the long term that this is probably going to become something of a problem, but I mean in the short term it's kind of hot."

"Marissa!"

"I'm sorry, I can't help it, the fact that you are stuck naked and all embarrassed and everything like that is making me horny. Don't be a hypocrite, situation reversed and I was stuck naked all the time you probably would be having fun with it."

Ethan had to admit that she had him there. "Maybe I would, but I would be taking it seriously and trying to find some type of solution to the problem, not just ogling you like some type of horny schoolgirl!"

Marissa looked down between Ethan's legs and smiled. "Well looks like I am not the only one who is getting turned on by the situation."

Ethan embarrassingly covered up his erection but he had already given himself away. As mortifying and humiliating as this entire situation was for him, he couldn't help but admit the fact that he was having an argument with his fully dressed girlfriend while he was completely buck naked was really getting the adrenaline flowing to the proper areas of his anatomy.

"That's beside the point!" Ethan said now blushing incredibly profusely and beginning to sweat.

"Yeah I can see how that would be a problem, not only are you finding this whole experience humiliating as hell, it's also making you as hot as hell. If you can't find some way to control yourself you're going to be going around completely buck naked sprouting a stiffy!"

"You're right; I can't go out in public like this!"

"Yeah and having guests over is going to be really awkward when my friends arrive later," Marissa said as she laughed.

"Having your friends over, you can't have your friends over with me like this! I couldn't imagine what could possibly be more embarrassing than all of your girlfriends coming over and seeing me like this."

"Merry Christmas," Meredith said as she opened the door followed by Amy, Susie, Felicia, Candace, Emily, Charlotte and Denise, who all pretty much stopped in their tracks and dropped everything they were carrying at the same exact moment as their eyes went wide.

"It's a naked dude with a boner!" Denise finally shouted as all of the girls began laughing hysterically as Ethan struggled to cover himself up and dove behind the couch.

"Who's the stripper?!" Candace said. "Well this is going to be a very Merry Christmas. I always knew that you go all out for the holidays Marissa, but you've outdone yourself this time."

"What are you all doing here?!" Ethan shouted as he hid sheepishly behind the couch.

"It's amazing the things you see when you arrive a little bit early," Susie said as she began laughing.

Marissa couldn't help but laugh. "I'm sorry; it's not really a funny situation, but Ethan you might as well come out from hiding behind the couch as everybody has already seen you."

"Holy crap that's Ethan," Charlotte said with a big smile. "I thought you said that Ethan was really shy, it looks like he has totally gotten over that!"

"We have kind of a situation here," Marissa said. "Maybe you should sit down for this one. It seems that Ethan has developed some type of allergy."

"An allergy, what type of allergy makes you run around completely buck naked like that?" Felicia asked.

"Well it seems that Ethan has some type of weird, possibly psychosomatic illness, where he is totally allergic to all forms of clothing," Marissa said.

"That sounds like something that you just made up like right now," Emily said. "Look Marissa if you want to have some kinky fun with your boyfriend and everything like that we understand, you don't have to make up these crazy off-the-wall notions that he is allergic to clothing."

"It's kind of true," Ethan said still crouching behind the couch, blushing profusely and trying to hide himself from all of Marissa's friends, who had the worst timing humanly possible.

"I can honestly say I have never heard of anything like that," Amy said shaking her head. "But I have to say it sounds rather interesting! Would you mind if I perhaps played the doctor for a moment?"

"Are you a licensed physician," Ethan said as Amy started approaching.

Amy got really right up into his face intimidating him. "Let's just say I know my way around human anatomy pretty well."

"I really don't want to be the private anatomy lesson of a bunch of women on Christmas day," Ethan said still crouching down and doing his best to hide from all of the women who were now on the other side of the couch staring directly at his ass, causing him to jump up and cover himself and dive on the other side of the couch.

"Well I have to admit it doesn't look like he is in this situation willingly," Candace said. "Normally when a guy wants to engage in some form of exhibitionism he isn't hiding at every turn."

"This doesn't have anything to do with that movie Snakes on a Plane does it?" Denise said.

"Oh he's the Snakes on a Plane guy isn't he," Meredith said.

"What did you tell all of your friends that the Snakes on a Plane movie gave me a traumatic episode," Ethan said.

"Well girls gossip sometimes Ethan, and I mean who gets such a visceral reaction from a movie that is so unrealistic and so ridiculous that something like that's never going to happen," Marissa said.

"Hey it could happen, not very likely I'll admit, but you know stranger things have happened, sort of like me being allergic to freaking clothing!" Ethan shouted feeling increasingly intimidated by the fact that he was now surrounded by fully dressed women on every side.

Meredith shook her head. "You know this would have been a great fundraiser for our sorority back in the day, sort of like when we used to go to those strip clubs together."

"You went to strip clubs?" Ethan asked looking at Marissa.

"Well hey it's not like guys are the only ones who go to strip clubs," Marissa said. "But it's not like I did it constantly, I was just curious a couple of times."

"If by a couple of times you mean every weekend for your entire college career, where the male strippers basically knew you as the best G string tipper," Amy said laughing. "They called you million-dollar Marissa because they thought that they would send their kids through college one day through all of the dollar bills that you put in their G strings."

Marissa blushed. "They're exaggerating of course, it wasn't every single weekend, I mean some weekends I actually did have to study, and then some weekends it was closed, like on holidays. Look don't judge me, there is nothing wrong with a woman enjoying and celebrating her own sexual exploits the way a guy would, well you know a normal guy, not a bashful one like you."

"So now you're saying I am abnormal," Ethan said shaking his head.

Marissa shook her head. "Well the situation you are in right now is certainly abnormal. I mean let's face as it's not every single day that a guy suddenly finds himself allergic to clothing, and on Christmas of all days!"

"Well it sounds like Marissa got what she wanted for Christmas," Meredith said as she started slapping all of the women five as they all started whistling and hollering and clapping. "And it looks like as her honored guests we get to enjoy the gift as well."

"And the gift is already unwrapped!" Candace said as she slapped her knees and began laughing hysterically.

Ethan shook his head. "I must have done something to really

embarrass somebody really horribly in a past life to be subjected to this."

"Look everybody Ethan's a little bit uptight and insecure about, you know the fact that he can't wear clothes, so let's not try to be weird about it," Marissa said. "Let's just treat this as an ordinary everyday situation. Just try to be mature and reasonable about this, and not just resort to screaming around like a bunch of crazy horny schoolgirls."

"Looks like it's Chippendale's night!" Amy shouted as she clapped her hands as all of the women started screaming and shouting and turning on the stereo to start playing loud strip club music.

"Kill me now!" Ethan shouted.

"Oh come on Ethan, it is not the worst thing in the world," Marissa said as she put her arm around him. "Just think when else have you ever had so much attention from so many attractive women at one time?"

Ethan tried his best to suck it up, but the truth is that he was the person who went out of his way not to seek attention or to be the center of attention, and now that he was the center of attention he found that there was no way of avoiding the situation.

"Let's get this Christmas party started!" Meredith shouted as all the women began whistling and clapping.

Ethan so wanted to crawl into a hole and die, or at least crawl into a hole and cover himself up with something so that everybody wouldn't be staring at him, but as much as he hated to admit it there was something exciting about the whole situation. He was still certainly no exhibitionist, but Marissa was right about one thing, he had never remembered any time when so many women were focusing their attention on him exclusively like that, and for a moment, as Marissa was looking over in his general direction, he almost thought he detected a hint of jealousy from her.

He had to admit that would be a first. He had always been extremely loyal to Marissa, and Marissa knew that he was extremely shy about asking anybody out or seeking attention from other women. In fact she was the one who asked him out after she got tired of waiting and hoping that he would make a move on her. If it were left up to him he would probably still be eternally single.

"Hey," Amy said as she came over to Ethan with a big smile

on her face. He didn't know exactly how to deal with a situation like this, as no woman had seen him naked before except for Marissa, so this was a new experience for him, a very public experience.

"Um, hey," Ethan said looking around to see if there was any way he could excuse himself from the situation, while trying not to be rude. Although how he could he be the rude one when all of these women were the ones staring at his naked body?

"You know I actually am a licensed physician, Dr. Amy Florentine," Amy said as she shook hands with Ethan with one hand, as he put the other hand to cover himself up between his legs.

"Nice to meet you," Ethan said desperately searching for any excuse for him to pull himself away from the situation without making it look like he was obviously trying to escape.

Amy had a big smile on her face. "So how's it going?"

Ethan was cringing now, as it seemed as though she were trying to make small talk with him as they were both beating around the bush over the fact that he was standing there completely buck naked.

"Well you know it's been better I suppose, having a little bit of a weird holiday," Ethan said as Amy nodded and took a sip of her drink.

"You know what encouraged me to become a doctor in the first place?" Amy said.

"A desire to help humanity?"

"Well sort of, but that wasn't the only motivation."

"The money?"

Amy nodded. "That's one good reason, but it's not the primary reason that I became a doctor. No Ethan, the reason why I became a doctor is I like the fact that it gave me unfettered access to the human body, both men and women, but especially men. Do you have any idea how many men I have seen naked Ethan?"

"I'm guessing it's quite a lot."

Ethan hated the fact that he was basically being interrogated while completely naked by a fully dressed woman, and not just that but a professional woman, a doctor.

Amy nodded. "And not all just in the medical profession, you're probably looking at me and thinking I'm an overachieving Asian woman with a tiger mom, probably pressured into becoming a doctor by her parents, but that wasn't true at all, I like everything about being a doctor, but what I really liked was getting to examine the human body up close and personal without any reservations."

"You don't say," Ethan said desperately looking for any excuse to get away from this situation, as he could see that Amy was enjoying every last moment of it.

"Look Ethan maybe I can examine you and see what is wrong with you, you know in a strictly professional sense and everything."

Ethan cringed and knew that he was blushing profusely again, but he didn't want to be rude.

"Well I actually already was examined by a doctor, Dr. Spinelli and everything," Ethan said, thinking back to his examination not that long before and how embarrassing that was, but how much less embarrassing that was than being examined by one of his girlfriend's personal friends.

"Yes but you see Ethan I am a dermatologist, as I specialize in skin, and right now you are showing a whole lot of skin," Amy said shaking her head. "Look I just want to examine your skin very carefully, I'll be gentle, don't worry, I'll be strictly professional and everything."

As Ethan looked Amy in the eyes she was smiling and looking really friendly and everything, and although he really would like to get this situation over with as quickly as possible, he figured that she was being nice offering her services for free like that, and he figured that maybe if he let her examine his skin that he would be able to get out of this situation sooner, so reluctantly he nodded and agreed.

As Amy took Ethan into the other room and started examining his skin Ethan found himself cringing and struggling not to laugh as Amy traced her fingers all over his skin, tickling him mercilessly.

"You should stand still, you're being very jumpy, I didn't realize you were so ticklish," Amy said.

"Are we almost done?" Ethan said, finding the whole situation extremely humiliating, even if she was a professional and a doctor.

"Just about, let me get some really good close-up looks," she said as she started feeling his ass and other parts of his body.

Finally Amy seemed to be completing his exam as she stood

there with her arms folded in front of him smiling.

"So what's up Doc," Ethan said as the two of them laughed.

"Well Ethan I have to say that in my professional medical opinion."

"Yes?"

She looked him directly in the eye, feeling like he was getting a stare down from her, before she shrugged her shoulders and laughed. "Honestly Ethan I don't have the slightest clue. I don't know if you are just faking this to get attention or what, but at any rate I am enjoying every moment of it, so whatever you are doing keep it up, I think you're going to be a very popular guy around here!"

Amy gave him a firm pat on the ass as she walked out of the room laughing and giggling the whole time.

"Ethan here you are, I was wondering where you went," Marissa said as she came into the room.

"Your friend the doctor gave me a free examination, but even she couldn't figure out what was wrong, and she's a medical professional."

"What you mean Amy?"

"Yeah of course Amy, why do you have more than one friend who is a doctor?"

"She told you that she was a doctor?"

"Yes, isn't she?"

"She wanted to be a doctor but then she dropped out of medical school because it was too much time and money to continue medical school. She loves playing doctor though, I'll say that much!"

As Marissa looked at Ethan standing there still completely naked and covering himself up she couldn't help but burst out laughing and he couldn't help but burst out laughing as well as Amy had really pulled a number over on him.

As Marissa went out into the room to mingle with her friends Ethan stood there feeling he had just been played for the fool and shaking his head. "That Amy, she may not be a doctor, but she's going places, where I don't know, but I'm sure that she is going to like wherever it is she is going."

7

Ethan had to admit that in a lot of ways he was socially ignorant, and now that he suddenly found himself in a naked situation like that he was realizing just how his social ignorance was perhaps backfiring on him. What Amy did would have been funny in a different context, but he had to admit that the whole thing made him feel especially embarrassed. At this point he just wanted to go hide for the rest of the night and not make any scenes.

"Ethan if you feel really uncomfortable I can ask my friends to leave," Marissa said as she came back in the room to see him. "I honestly never expected them to arrive so early, and you'll forgive Amy, she's just a very curious person."

"And by curious you mean a perv?"

"Well I don't think that is completely fair, I mean sure maybe she was a little bit deceptive and everything like that, but it's only natural to be curious when you have a naked person around. You're going to have to get used to people seeing you like this Ethan, if this condition is going to be a long-standing problem you're going to have to get used to it sooner or later and the sooner the better. Anyway I don't want to leave my friends alone for too long; they can sometimes get out of hand."

Ethan swallowed deeply out of nervousness, as he thought about the possibilities of Marissa's friends getting even more out of hand than they already were. How much more out of hand could they possibly get?

Ethan had to admit that he knew that Marissa ran with something of a wild crowd, but he had never met all of her friends like that all at once. What were the odds that they were all going to go to Hawaii at the same time that she would?

Ethan went to his suitcase and dug through his piles of now useless clothing until he found the small box at the bottom of his suitcase. He opened it up and looked at the diamond ring that he had inside. His goal had always been to propose to Marissa on Christmas, but under the circumstances he didn't know how he could possibly go through with it. Could he really get down on one knee completely buck naked and in all seriousness ask Marissa if she wanted to marry him?

Then he had suddenly a weird thought, a troubling thought, but one that he could not get out of his head. Suddenly he saw an image of himself walking down the aisle with Marissa, her in her bridal gown and him completely and utterly buck naked. Was that the type of future that he was going to have with her? He figured that she deserved better than something like that. No, until he get this situation resolved satisfactorily he wasn't going to make any long-term plans or make Marissa feel any obligation to go along with those plans, even though the way she was reacting he felt that she probably would say yes to him one way or another, in fact she would probably be quite enthusiastic at the idea of a naked wedding, that was the type of woman that she was!

However as he thought to himself what he was going to do for Christmas now, seeing as that was going to be his gift to her, he thought he would have to go to plan B. He didn't just get her a ring, he had got her some rather skimpy lingerie, which under the circumstances he would feel weird giving to her in front of all of her friends, so that would have to wait until later.

Ethan looked at himself in the mirror, once again cringing over the fact that he was completely naked when there were other people in the house like that. He looked at his naked body for a couple of moments. He had never really given it a good examine before. How strange it is you can be in a body for several decades of your life and never really give it a good looking over like that. Obviously he had looked at his naked body before but he had never really really looked at it.

As he looked at his body and thought to himself that maybe he was stuck like this forever, he thought to himself it could be worse, at least he wasn't that ugly. Then on the other hand if he was stuck like this forever maybe it would be better to be ugly, because then people wouldn't be staring at him everywhere he goes.

But once again he found it weird that this was the first time he ever seriously looked at his naked body before. Maybe he really was a bit uptight, and maybe even a bit of a prude, at least compared to Marissa. Well definitely compared to her he certainly was, but that was true of most people. But that was one of the things he admired about her, Marissa didn't have any shame about expressing her own sexuality, and she didn't have any problems with her body. She was the exhibitionist, he was just the opposite.

As he continued staring at himself he swallowed deeply and then thought of another gift that he could potentially give to Marissa in the meantime, although he didn't know if he could work up the resolve to do it. He really wanted her to have a Merry Christmas and then not feel guilty about his situation, but what he was thinking about doing was beyond embarrassing.

"The things we do for love," he said as he inhaled deeply and started walking out into the living room where Marissa was with all of her friends.

"Well well well it looks like somebody has come out of hiding," Meredith said as all eyes turned to Ethan as he once again began blushing and cringing. As all of the women's eyes were boring into him, he could never remember a time when he was subject to such a relentless female gaze like that, and it felt even more intimidating than he even thought when he first walked out there.

"Marissa I had a really great gift that I wanted to give to you for Christmas, but under the circumstances I feel that it might have to wait until another time, but in the meantime I really want you to have the most Merry Christmas possible," Ethan said. "And I want your friends to be happy as well. So my Christmas gift to you is that for the rest of the night I am your own personal naked butler."

Ethan stood there for a moment surrounded by awkward silence as he slowly saw a devious looking smile appearing across Marissa's face.

"This is just going to be like all of those old times in college," Meredith said as she began clapping and laughing as all of the women began whistling and hollering.

For a moment Ethan had to admit that he felt really idiotic, extremely silly about the whole affair, but then he went into the kitchen and started preparing drinks, which he then came out and began serving to the women as they all smiled and toasted to him.

As Ethan walked around serving glasses of champagne to fully dressed women who were staring at his naked body, he had to admit that it was a certainly new feeling that he had never experienced before, and it was not as terrible as he thought it would be. As he saw the smiles on the faces of all the women that he greeted and brought drinks to he thought that this was actually a rather nice thing to do, it was nice that the women were being able to relax and enjoy his naked body like that. And although he was still feeling extremely self-conscious, as he saw the women continue to laugh and snicker and everything like that, he realized it was a very relaxed atmosphere, and there was something about that which made him feel good.

"You know this is sort of like strip club night in our college, but there's something more, I don't know, wholesome about it," Candace said. "Okay it's not wholesome, not at all, but there is something kind of nice about having a naked man at our disposal like this."

Ethan tried not to act like he was eavesdropping, but as he saw all of the women smiling and relaxing he realized that he hadn't ever seen something like this before. It wasn't like the crazy atmosphere of a strip club; it was just a bunch of well-dressed women, in their Christmas finest, safely and calmly enjoying having a naked man waiting on them hand and foot.

As he continued going around he had to try his hardest not to get an erection, but he found that something about the situation was making him feel excited. Although Marissa was often one to take charge in the bedroom, he always felt that he was the one who was supposed to initiate everything, but now he was in a more passive and somewhat more submissive role and it actually felt kind of nice, he almost felt that the pressure was being taken off, that he was under no obligation to do anything except let the women enjoy the fact that he was there.

Every time a woman would beckon him over to get her another drink the feeling started increasing. Performing all of these little acts of servitude towards women, while completely and utterly naked, he never felt more vulnerable and exposed, but at the same time he never felt the situation was more right. Something about this just seemed natural to him, something about it seemed, he didn't know how to put it into words, but he was feeling good about what was going on.

Amazingly, and he didn't know quite exactly how it was even possible, as the night went on the women simply started treating him as just another Christmas decoration, like the tree or the wreath or the stockings, or like a big naked Christmas tree light, a red one obviously, because of all the blushing.

"You know Marissa you really do have a very gracious boyfriend here, and I think that I can speak for everyone here when I say that he has been the perfect butler," Emily said as she raised her glass in a toast to the other women who raised their glasses as well.

"Just happy to be of service," Ethan said, although he knew he must be blushing profusely, as this was probably the single most embarrassing night of his life, as now every single one of Marissa's friends had seen him completely naked, not just once, but continuously all night long. Even if he was eventually able to put his clothing back on every time he saw them from now on they would be able to picture him naked, and he couldn't do the same to them, and it really was a very weird feeling.

"I guess I should go and get the Christmas dinner ready," Ethan said as all of the women sat around the table and he brought out a large turkey and put it down in front of them.

"You really are a lucky woman Marissa, you have a boyfriend who not only cooks really well, but he knows how to look good doing it!" Susie said as all of the women began laughing once again.

Ethan slowly and carefully went around cutting off pieces of the turkey and serving it to the women, who all smiled and got a good look at him every time he brought them something.

"I would just like to say thank you for all of the free meat that is on display tonight," Felicia said. "And as you may have guessed I am not talking exclusively about the turkey!"

Everybody at the table laughed, including Ethan. As he was getting more involved in the absurdity of the situation he found himself and he could see the humor in it, even though he still knew that he was blushing profusely and that nothing was going to stop that anytime soon.

"Yeah this has probably been the best Christmas I can remember in a long time," Candace said. "I mean it's like we got our own personal strip show, and we got somebody waiting on us hand and foot all night. I don't think that I have ever experienced being served food by a naked man before!"

"Until this morning I would have said the same thing," Marissa said as she winked and laughed as everybody started oohing and ahing.

Ethan could barely contain himself now, as he knew that Marissa must have been totally power tripping on this. If her fantasy was to have a man serving her breakfast naked, surely a man serving her and all of her girlfriends dinner naked, Christmas dinner on top of that, must have been the icing on the cake, and he knew that as he looked her directly in the eye that this present had been more than satisfactory to her.

At the same time he then found himself relieved that he was

finally able to sit down at the table with all of the women and finally cover up the more private parts of his anatomy with the dinner table and the tablecloth. As he began eating the turkey he had to admit that he had cooked it rather well, and that he really was a pretty good chef. In fact it tasted so good for a moment it even momentarily distracted him from the fact that he was eating dinner completely buck naked with a group of well-dressed women like it was the most normal thing in the world.

Maybe I can get used to this after all, Ethan thought to himself. But as he saw everybody looking up from their food to stare at him, knowing that this could be the case wherever he went from now on, he quickly disabused himself of that thought. It was one thing to be naked around Marissa and her friends; it was another thing to be naked in public at large.

Marissa raised her glass and began hitting it with a fork as everybody got quiet. "Everyone I would just like to say that this has been probably the most interesting Christmas that I have ever had, and I think that I owe it all to my excellent boyfriend Ethan. Not only is he an excellent cook, but he makes for a pretty good naked butler!"

All of the women began snickering and laughing, especially Amy, who seemed to have that evil smirk on her face at having been able to trick Ethan earlier, but at the moment he didn't even really care about that.

"So I would just like to raise my glass in toast to Ethan, the best boyfriend I have ever had and the love of my life," Marissa said as she and everybody else at the table raised their glasses.

"To Ethan!" all of the women said as they clinked glasses together.

Once dinner was over Ethan finished clearing the table and they all decided to have dessert together.

"Well I would say that I didn't need any dessert after the really sweet night that I have had," Marissa said. "But I know that Ethan makes great dessert as well, so dig in everybody."

As all of the women sat there eating their ice cream Ethan once again thought to himself that this was crazy, there he was sitting at a table with a bunch of eight well-dressed women eating ice cream while he was sitting there completely naked doing likewise.

Once dessert was over it was time to exchange gifts.

"Well Ethan I suppose that the gift I got you might not be the best gift under the circumstances right now, and it is sort of the opposite of the gift that you gave me, but here you go, Merry Christmas," Marissa said as she handed him a Christmas sweater.

"Thank you, it's extremely lovely," Ethan said as he felt his eyes began watering as he hugged the sweater close against his naked flesh but could feel it burning against his skin before he put it back down. "I actually got you something clothing related as well but I think I will have to give it to you later, as it's a little bit skimpy."

"Somehow I doubt it's as skimpy as what you are wearing," Amy said as all of the women began laughing and enjoying themselves again.

And as Ethan sat there surrounded by well-dressed women staring at his naked body, he found that he continued crying, and crying, and crying, and soon he realized that he just couldn't stop, so he just kept on crying as Marissa came by and patted him on the back assuring him that everything would be okay.

He wanted to believe that as well, but in his heart of hearts as he continued sitting there naked on display for the entire world to see, he couldn't bring himself to believe it and continued crying.

It had been a long and very exciting and strange Christmas day, and he could see now that it was going to be a very long, interesting and strange Christmas night.

8

After Marissa's friends went home for the night the two of them sat in bed together for a long time not saying anything particularly, both sort of having a moment of silence, because neither of them knew exactly what to say under the circumstances.

"But don't worry Ethan I am sure that whatever this is it will wear off eventually, I mean maybe it will just go away when the New Year comes," Marissa said.

"You mean it's just going to magically go away when New Year's Eve comes, that this entire allergy is just going to somehow disappear like it was never there in the first place," Ethan said. "Why on earth would it just suddenly go away like that? Why did it just suddenly appear out of nowhere like that? Am I going crazy or something, maybe it really is psychosomatic?"

Marissa had to admit that now she was feeling guilty, as she realized that she hadn't told Ethan the thing that she had been withholding from him all this time, the fact that it was her fault that he was in that situation, and she felt even more guilty over the fact that she was enjoying every single moment of it.

"Ethan I have a confession to make, there was something I have not told you about this whole situation," Marissa said sort of twiddling her thumbs and not exactly sure how to say it.

"What is it that you have a new kink that you would like to try?"

Marissa gritted her teeth. "Ethan this is very hard for me to admit, but I feel that this is all my fault."

Ethan shook his head. "Don't feel guilty about this, it's not your fault that I seem to have some type of psychosomatic illness, that I'm screwed up in the head. If anything you have been nothing but supportive, teasing me relentlessly perhaps, enjoying every moment of it, but you have been as supportive as any woman that I could have ever hoped for in a situation like this. If I had to be naked forever around somebody I would want it to be you."

"Oh Ethan, that's the sweetest thing you have said to me all day," Marissa said as she kissed him on the cheek as she began ringing her fingers. "Which is why I can't keep this from you any longer, you see it actually is my fault that you can't wear clothing."

"What are you saying, that you played a joke on me, put itching powder in my clothing or something?"

"Not exactly, I know you're probably going to be that really rational objective skeptic type that you tend to be, but you see when we were on the plane ride here, remember when we saw all of those shooting stars and everything like that?"

"Yes I do remember, but don't worry you pointing out that there were meteor storms going on wasn't going to give me some type of nervous reaction that's going to make me allergic to my clothing, that just wouldn't make any logical sense."

"No Ethan, it's not that, you see when all of those shooting stars were going across the sky I sort of made kind of a wish."

"You wished on a shooting star?"

Marissa nodded. "Yes, I wished on a shooting star that just for one week you wouldn't be able to wear clothing. Now don't be angry at me Ethan, I mean how was I supposed to know that it was going to come true?! I have wished on a shooting star many times before and nothing I have ever wished for has ever come true like this, especially not something so weirdly specific."

Ethan looked at her for a moment before smiling and bursting out in laughter.

"What's so funny Ethan?" Marissa asked.

"Nothing Marissa, I just found that extremely funny, that's a really funny joke you are playing on me there. So you are saying that the reason why I can't wear clothing is because you made a wish on a shooting star?"

Marissa nodded. "Yes Ethan I am, and I am so sorry, I totally didn't mean for this to happen."

Ethan grabbed her by the hands. "Marissa you are completely blameless in this, I didn't even know you made a wish on a shooting star, so how could I have a psychosomatic illness resulting from that when I didn't even know about it?"

"Because it's not psychosomatic Ethan, you can't wear clothing because I made the wish on the shooting star and the wish came true!"

Ethan laughed again.

"Why are you laughing?" Marissa said as she stood up with her hands on her hips in a really defiant manner, as she didn't really like being laughed at like that.

"Nothing, it's just you are suggesting that the reason why I can't wear clothing is because of what, magic? Is that what you are really suggesting, that I can't wear clothing because of some type of magical wish on a shooting star?" Ethan continued laughing until he was practically in hysterics.

"You think that I'm just some type of irrational crazy person because I believe in magic wishes don't you?" Marissa said shaking her head.

"Well come on Marissa, let's be logical about this, you really believe that the reason why I can't wear clothing is because you made a wish on a shooting star? I know that you believe in some crazy thing sometimes, but that has to really take the cake. I really love your imagination but I think that sometimes it runs away with you."

Marissa frowned. "I don't think it's funny Ethan, can't you be a little bit open-minded to the possibility that there are some things in this world that we don't understand?"

"Look I'm open-minded about lots of things, but the idea that I can't wear clothing because of a magical wish on a shooting star, I'm sorry but that's a little bit too far even for my taste." He sat there shaking his head and laughing to himself at how gullible that Marissa was being.

Now Marissa was positively angry as she pulled the blanket off of him as he covered up his naked body.

"Hey what gives," Ethan said, now blushing once again.

"You know what I think is really funny, you know what I think is absolutely screaming hilarious, you can't wear clothing!"

"Marissa what are you doing," he said standing up and covering his genitals with his hands as he started walking back.

"I'm saying that I think that this is the most screamingly hilarious thing that I have ever seen in my entire life. I mean my boyfriend can't wear clothing, I must have hit the freaking jackpot, it's like I won the lottery! I mean what is funnier than the idea of a guy who has to go naked everywhere he goes, a guy never getting to wear clothing again. Naked naked naked naked!"

"Come on stop it now," Ethan said as he was once again blushing profusely and shaking a little bit at the knees.

"What's the matter, you don't like the fact that everybody can see you completely buck naked! Hey everybody look at Ethan the amazing naked man. He can't even put on clothing, something that everyone else in the world can do." Marissa started pulling at the fabric of her clothing, at the little black negligée that Ethan had given her earlier in the night, and strutting about the house. "Look at me, I may not be very heavily dressed but I get to wear clothing! It may be scantily clad but it's more than you're getting to wear!"

As Ethan stood there in front of Marissa, strutting about in this skimpy black negligée that he had given her earlier in the night, mocking her with the very article of clothing that he had given her, that was when he found himself even more embarrassed as he felt all of the blood rushing to his genitals as he quickly became as hard as a rock.

The two of them stood there staring at each other as a big smile grew across Marissa's face. "Well well well, looks like I finally got a reaction out of Mr. cool, calm and collected! Somebody looks like they are very happy to see me, and I think that somebody might be secretly happy that they can't wear clothing because they are naked naked naked naked!"

For a moment Ethan looked furious as the two of them stared each other down, until the next thing they knew they were making out and Marissa was diving on top of Ethan and screeching like a maniac.

"So a magical wish on a shooting star, huh," Ethan said as the two of them laid in bed after a marathon session of lovemaking.

Marissa nodded. "Yep, this is all the result of one magical wish on a shooting star. I know it sounds crazy Ethan —"

Ethan put his finger over her lips. "No no, I was wrong to be narrow-minded. Maybe this is the result of wishing on a shooting star, maybe it isn't, but one way or another I think that you definitely got your wish didn't you?"

Marissa smiled. "Are you telling me you're not enjoying it as well?"

"Well I know I'm enjoying this part of it, I don't think we have ever had as intense lovemaking before this had happened, and I do appreciate that aspect of it, but I certainly can't spend the rest of my life naked in public like that, I would have to be forced to move to a nudist colony or something!"

Marissa started giggling. "I'm sorry, just the thought of you living in a nudist colony is too entertaining to contemplate. Going from wearing fancy suits all the time to having to go around buck naked with everybody else buck naked looking at you, I feel like making another wish on a shooting star!"

"But this is only going to be temporary, if you really did make a wish on a shooting star and that is the reason why I can't wear clothing as soon as the New Year comes around I should be able to wear clothing again, right?"

"Well Ethan I have never really made a wish on a shooting star that has come true before, but assuming all of the rules of that follow logically with the rest of what has happened, then yes, I suppose by New Year's Day you will finally be able to put on some clothing."

"But in the meantime I guess the rest of our vacation is going to be an indoor vacation, seeing as I can't put on any clothing now for the rest of the week."

Marissa smirked. "I guess I hadn't considered that when I made my wish, but then on the other hand when I made my wish I had no idea that it was actually going to come true! I was thinking that maybe I could make another wish on a shooting star and that would cancel out the first one, but it doesn't look like there are any shooting stars out tonight, and besides I think that your heart has to really be in it, and as much as I want to help you Ethan I have to admit that if I wished on a shooting star tonight for you to no longer be cursed to be naked, well I have to be honest I don't think I would truly mean it or want it to come true. But I am sure that we can still have a fun holiday here in the tropics of Hawaii right here on this beach."

"Or at least in the cabin anyway," Ethan said as he looked out the window.

"Well you know Ethan the beach that our cabin happens to be located on is clothing optional."

"What are you saying?"

"I'm saying that there is no excuse for you to be cooped up in the house all day, you'll get cabin fever, and seeing as you're already having an allergic reaction to clothing I don't think you want that on top of everything else!"

Ethan nodded and smiled. "Marissa I have been very good about this, I think you'll agree, I have managed to put up with being completely buck naked in front of all of your girlfriends, and will probably never be able to look them in the eye without blushing for the rest of my life, but it's going to be a really really cold day in this tropical paradise before you see me walking out naked on a nude beach. Hell will freeze over before you see me doing that."

As Ethan sat there in bed crossing his arms Marissa knew that that was the end of the discussion and that there was no moving him on that question. He had put his foot down and that was final.

9

"Please Marissa, you know that this is just too much for me," Ethan said as Marissa started dragging him towards the door.

Marissa shook her head. "Don't be such a baby, come on now, you already been seen naked by me and all of my girlfriends, what's the big deal about a bunch of strangers on the beach seeing you naked?"

"But what if I run into somebody that I know?"

"Ethan virtually every single person that we know aside from my girlfriends who came on this trip with us, who have already seen every last inch of your naked ass and every other nook and cranny of your anatomy, virtually pretty much everyone we know lives in New York. What are the odds that somebody is going to run into you on a nude beach in Hawaii on the other side of the world? The odds are so infinitesimally small that they're pretty much zero. I don't think it's a good excuse to stay indoors all day. We are here on a tropical Hawaiian vacation, it's a beautiful 80° day, perfect weather for the beach, and just think, you're going to get the best tan of your life!"

Ethan gritted his teeth. He knew that Marissa could be very persuasive when she got to arguing, and he knew that it wasn't likely that they were going to go on another tropical Hawaiian vacation anytime soon, but at the same time the prospect that he would see somebody who potentially knew him, however infinitesimally small those odds were, was purely terrifying to him, and what if some random person on the beach happened to get a picture of him and it found its way on the Internet, once something was on the Internet it was on there forever.

"Are you going to get naked as well?" Ethan said with a big evil smile on his face, as he figured that maybe he would call her bluff.

"Clothing optional doesn't mean that you have to get naked, it means that clothing is just one of many options," Marissa said.

"Come on, you're like a budding exhibitionist, don't you want to go running naked on the beach like that?"

"I'm not uptight about my body, but I'm no exhibitionist the way you seem to think I am, okay so maybe sometimes I'm an exhibitionist, but I don't know I've never been on a nude beach before. Plus I really like this little black thong bikini that I bought for just such an occasion, and I would really like to show it off."

Marissa held up the skimpy black bikini and Ethan had to admit something about that was extremely hot. Although he wouldn't admit it to Marissa if she twisted his arm behind his back, the prospect of going on the beach with her in that black bikini while he was completely buck naked was already getting him excited, but he didn't want to make it so obvious, so he decided that he would play the reluctant accessory.

"It's okay, you don't have to get naked, I understand that even somebody like you can have some reservations," Ethan said as Marissa changed into her little black bikini. Seeing her naked briefly, just while she was changing, was enough to excite Ethan's passion, but as soon as she had that clothing on again once again he felt like he was the one in the vulnerable position. Even though that skimpy thong bikini didn't leave a whole lot to the imagination, it still left more to the imagination than Ethan's birthday suit did, and just that little bit of covering that she had over him sent him a powerful message that she was the one in charge.

"Well it's not just that Ethan, but I wasn't exactly planning to go on the beach alone today," Marissa said as she opened the door as all of her girlfriends from the night before were standing there wearing various different bathing suits, from one pieces to bikinis to full coverings.

"Of course all of your girlfriends are coming with us, and of course they are all fully dressed," Ethan said shaking his head and feeling his legs began to shake as he knew that he was blushing and covered in goosebumps already.

"Naked man ahoy!" Meredith shouted as all of the women began laughing.

"Well this is going to be a very very long day," Ethan said shaking his head.

"Oh don't be a baby Ethan, I am sure that there are going to be plenty of people other than you naked and that no one's even going to hardly take any notice of you, don't get such a big ego already," Marissa said. "In fact you're probably going to make me jealous with all of the naked women that you're going to be seeing on the beach today. You're going to be drowning in naked women, just suffocating in them."

Ethan had to admit that maybe Marissa had a point; maybe he would be in a virtual flesh paradise. If everybody was naked then it was pretty much the same as if nobody was naked, because he wouldn't stand out like a sore thumb, or in this case a blushing red tomato. Maybe it wouldn't be so bad after all.

"It's been an hour and I haven't seen a single other naked person yet," Ethan said as they laid down on their blankets sunbathing as groups of women went by pointing and laughing at

Ethan as he covered himself up and blushed.

"The first rule of a naked beach is that everybody that you want to see naked is definitely going to be wearing clothing," Amy said. "And you know a nude beach is just a whole lot of naked guys hoping to see a whole lot of naked girls."

"But I haven't seen a single other naked guy in this whole place, not that I really want to see any other naked guys, but at least then I wouldn't be the only one," Ethan said. He had to admit the fact that they had been on the beach all day and that the only one naked was him made him feel even more naked than he had been before, more exposed and vulnerable, as though he were a sideshow freak for the entire world to gawk at.

"I don't think you would ever survive as a woman with all of the constant sexual objectification that we receive," Candace said. "And that's with us keeping our clothing on. You're just not used to the idea of women seeing you as a sex object, as a bunch of flesh. But if you can't put on any clothing I guess you're going to have to get used to it aren't you, Mr. naked man."

All of the women sort of nodded and voiced agreement with Candace, and it made Ethan feel like all of the women were ganging up on him. It's like hadn't they ever seen a naked guy in a vulnerable position like that before? And then he realized to himself that maybe they hadn't. He had always taken female nudity as the norm for granted, he never thought of what a different experience it must be for women to see a guy feeling naked and self-conscious about his own nudity.

"Hey would any of you like to play volleyball," a woman said as she came by wearing a one-piece bathing suit staring directly at Ethan. "I just saw you ladies over here with your naked male companion and I thought I would say hi."

"My name is Ethan," Ethan said, realizing that now he no longer even was addressed by his name, he was just that naked guy, arm candy for the ladies. Maybe he really was learning something about sexual objectification after all, and it was a strange feeling for a guy to experience.

"My name is Pam and I just thought that maybe you would all like to play a game of volleyball with us," Pam said as she pointed to some of her friends, all of whom happened to be wearing clothing.

Ethan had to admit he felt somewhat self-conscious at the idea of jumping around playing sports with all of his bits and pieces out on display, so he was going to just politely tell Pam that they were just enjoying a day of sunbathing.

"Naked guy volleyball, sounds like a great idea!" Marissa said as all of the women began high-fiving each other and the decision was made before Ethan could get a word in edgewise.

As they set up a volleyball net Ethan had to admit that he felt weird being the only one naked in the volleyball game, and he could see several women on the other team staring over at him smirking to themselves, and a couple were pointing and laughing. It was making him feel extremely self-conscious once again, but he felt that he had to suck it up and not let it bother him, even though he had to admit it was incredibly embarrassing.

For the next hour or so they played volleyball in the hot sun until Ethan's team had claimed victory.

"No fair, I was distracted looking at, well I was just distracted by Ethan," Pam said. "I'm sorry it's hard to concentrate on playing a game when you have a guy with his meat and two vegetables just flailing back and forth like that!"

All of the women began bursting out laughing, including Marissa, who was just eating this all up because it was just another opportunity for her to power trip over the fact that her boyfriend was the one who wasn't getting to wear any pants.

Ethan had to admit that he could take a joke as well as the next guy, but this was getting to be too much. It was weird being the constant butt of everybody's jokes just because you're naked. He didn't realize how much being naked changed your life, and as he thought about this more deeply he was glad that soon New Year's would be here and this would all be over with soon enough.

But what if it wasn't? Did he really honestly believe that this was all because of a wish that Marissa had made on a shooting star? The more he thought about it the more absurd that sounded. What if New Year's Day came and he was still unable to wear clothing, then what would he do? He couldn't exactly get on the airplane completely buck naked and go back to New York in January.

He didn't have long to worry about that however before he heard a loud female voice bursting out hysterically laughing.

"Oh my God Ethan Stanhope, I'd recognized that ass

anywhere," the woman said as Ethan turned around to see that standing there was Tricia, his ex-girlfriend of many years back, a relationship where things did not end very well.

"Tricia?!" Ethan said as he covered up his genitals and began blushing. He had always found her extremely intimidating, and for a while they had been serious, serious enough that he had even thought about proposing to her, until they realized that there were too many fundamental differences between them, namely the fact that Tricia was a little bit status obsessed and always thought that she was better than everybody.

"Well well well, you don't seem to be as shy as I remember you, then on the other hand you are blushing, which makes me think that you are the same old Ethan," Tricia said. "But I never thought I would run into you on a nude beach of all places! I mean you're the last person I could ever picture being on a nude beach, this is pretty rich!"

Tricia was standing there fully dressed in what looked like a lot of expensive designer clothing, which was just making Ethan feel even more humiliated by the situation, emasculated even.

"Hello Tricia," Marissa said as she walked over. Marissa knew of the history between them and she never really liked Tricia very much, and sometimes she even found herself jealous of Tricia, even though she was the one with Ethan now, which she emphasized by putting her arm around him.

"Well I can see who wears the pants in this relationship," Tricia said laughing, as Ethan found himself looking at his toes and feeling extremely humiliated by her mocking. It wasn't the same as when Marissa was laughing, her laughing and teasing weren't cruel like Tricia's. Even when he was fully dressed he had a hard time looking Tricia in the eyes, now that he was standing there completely naked, vulnerable and exposed like that, it was just destroying him.

"Ethan is a man who is not intimidated by a successful and independent woman who knows what she wants," Marissa said.

Tricia snorted. "That's not the way I remember things. Well Ethan it looks like you have gone from shy uptight guy, never willing to make a move or show initiative, to being the naked arm candy of a real estate agent."

"I love Marissa, and I won't have you say anything bad about her," Ethan said, still having a hard time attempting to make eye contact with Tricia.

"Well I can see what she likes about you," Tricia said laughing. "I had a hard time getting you naked in the privacy of the bedroom with the lights off, and now here she has you parading around naked on a nude beach for everybody to see. Like I said, we can see who wears the pants in this relationship."

Ethan could see that Tricia was power tripping like crazy, in a way that Marissa would never do. Sure Marissa liked to power trip over the fact that he was naked, but she never made it a mean-spirited thing, but Tricia on the other hand, was reveling in the fact that Ethan was clearly naked and humiliated in public.

"Let me just get a picture of the happy couple to remember you by, standing there naked and blushing away as always," Tricia said as she snapped a picture. "Anyway enjoy the rest of the holiday season, maybe I will see you around, although I think that I have already seen everything there is to see."

As Tricia walked off laughing, Ethan had to admit that this was perhaps the most humiliating moment of his life. Not only had Tricia emasculated him in front of his girlfriend and all of her girlfriends, but now she had a picture to remember the occasion by.

Marissa shook her head. "Don't let her get to you Ethan, she's just jealous that she isn't with you anymore. You know I will always love you for who you are, clothing, no clothing or anything in between. The clothes don't make the man, the man makes the man, and as far as I am concerned you have the best character of anybody that I had ever seen, and it takes a lot of guts for you to come out here and be naked and exposed like that. I'm proud of you Ethan, you didn't let her get to you."

But the thing that made Ethan feel ashamed is that for all of Marissa's words of praise, Tricia had gotten to him, right now he just wanted to go bury himself in a hole and hide from the world once again, but he didn't want to lose face, so he simply hugged Marissa and hoped that he wouldn't run into Tricia for the rest of the day, and hopefully not for the rest of his life afterwards.

"Come on, it's getting late," Marissa said not long afterwards, as they stood on the beach watching the sunset together. It was a beautiful romantic moment, but Ethan couldn't bring himself to enjoy it in the same way that Marissa was, because he knew somewhere out there was Tricia smiling to herself and laughing at him.

"Let's go home," Ethan said and they began walking back towards the cabin, with Ethan not quite so confident as before, and given that he was completely buck naked before as he was now, that was really saying something.

10

"Come on Ethan, this is our last day in Hawaii, we may not be able to go to a lot of the tourist attractions that aren't clothing optional, but at least let's enjoy our last day here in Hawaii, soon we are going to be back in the cold of New York," Marissa said. "Ever since you ran into Tricia on the beach you have been cooped up in this cabin for the last couple of days, we have wasted pretty much our entire vacation. Not that I haven't been enjoying all of the naked fun that we have been having here in the cabin, but it would be nice to be out in the sun and sand. What did we come to a tropical paradise for if we weren't going to enjoy that?"

"Well maybe if somebody hadn't wished on a shooting star that I had to be buck naked all the time," Ethan said before catching his tongue. "I'm sorry, I didn't mean it like that, I know you didn't intend for this to happen. I am sure that it was just an innocent wish that you made while you were horny."

"No, you are right Ethan, this was our vacation opportunity of a lifetime and I ruined it because of, but I guess for reasons that I couldn't have foreseen, but it still my fault and I feel bad about that. I'm not going to bug you to come out on the beach with me today, but I am hoping that we can at least enjoy New Year's together later at the party this evening out on the beach. Do you think you could at least do that for me Ethan?"

Ethan nodded. "I'll just be glad when the New Year comes and I can finally put on clothing again," he said as he swallowed deeply, as he wasn't still sure whether he fully believed it himself. His greatest fear was that midnight would come and he would still be unable to put on clothing, then he knew that he really was in serious trouble. But at least for the next few hours he still could live in hope.

Marissa kissed him on the cheek. "I'm going to go to the beach with some of my girlfriends and everything like that, but don't worry I won't be out all day. I am sure that you can find something to entertain yourself with here, can't you?"

"I'm sure I'll manage," Ethan said as Marissa left the room. Ethan started flipping through the television channels and saw that there was a pay-per-view Playboy channel, but something about the idea of ordering a bunch of movies full of naked women seemed kind of ridiculous under the circumstances. In fact it seemed like a weird thing for any guy to do after everything he had been through. He couldn't help but laugh to himself about that.

Ethan then went to his suitcase where he tried putting on his clothing, only to find that it was still burning his skin. In resignation he put the clothing back in the suitcase, as it seemed like this clothing wasn't the problem. He had washed all of his clothes numerous times thinking that maybe that was the cause of the allergic reaction. He had put on the sweater that Marissa had gotten him, only for it to have the same reaction. Marissa even went down to the store and bought him some new clothing and that all had the same reaction, so it had nothing to do with the clothing not having been washed sufficiently.

"I guess I'm naked until midnight now," Ethan said as he reached into his suitcase and took out the diamond ring that he had bought for Marissa and shook his head.

After everything they had been through could he really get down on one knee and ask Marissa to marry him? He knew that Marissa loved him, and that he certainly loved her, but with the future so uncertain he didn't know exactly what to say to her in a situation like that. Was he supposed to ask her will you take me to be your naked groom?

The more he thought about the possibility of popping the question, the more ridiculous it seemed to him. No, it would have to wait; he wouldn't be proposing like he had planned to on Christmas or on New Year's either. Besides where would he hide the ring on his body when he didn't even have any pockets? The more he thought about his situation the more absurd it seemed to him.

"I may not be proposing, but I am certainly going to make sure that Marissa has a New Year's to remember," he said as he started preparing a big meal for Marissa, her favorite meal of roast lamb, which would be a nice surprise for when she got home.

When Marissa arrived home a few hours later with all of her girlfriends Ethan was standing there with a feast fit for a king, or at least a Queen and all of her royal lady subjects.

"Ethan what is this?" Marissa said as she came in with her friends.

"Well I figured for our last night in Hawaii I would cook you a nice dinner and serve it to you," Ethan said.

"Naked butler part two!" Meredith shouted as all of the other girls began whistling and hollering, and Ethan realized what his role was for the next couple of hours at least.

"Ethan this is one of the nicest surprises ever, thank you," Marissa said as she kissed him on the lips and he began serving dinner.

Dinner was a quiet affair, with few people even commenting on the fact that Ethan was naked, although every time he was in sight of Marissa or her girlfriends he could see that they were all smiling and smirking and trying hard not to giggle. But once again there was something nice about being quietly subservient to the women like that, it once again felt really right to him somehow, as though he had somehow found his natural role that he had been resisting and avoiding his whole life.

"I would just like to propose yet another toast to my fabulous boyfriend Ethan," Marissa said at the end of the meal as she raised her glass. "We have been through a lot together, but nothing like what we have went through together in the last week. Ethan it has been a wild ride, and I think that we have both had a lot of fun, but I am sure that you will be glad that in just a short while you will finally be able to put on clothing again. I would just like to say that no matter what happens, whether you are able to get dressed in another hour or have to spend the rest of your life completely buck naked, I'm with you for the long haul and I wouldn't have it any other way. Clothed, naked, it's all good, I love you!"

Ethan wiped away a tear as he kissed Marissa on the forehead. As he looked in Marissa's eyes he could see the genuine love that was coming from them, and it was only really then at that moment that he truly realized that she would be with him through the thick and thin, no matter what would happen. If she had to spend the rest of her life with everybody staring at her because she had a naked boyfriend she would be willing to put up with that, although in her case it probably would be a case of enjoyment, but he still felt good that she didn't judge him by the clothing that he wore but by the person he was deep down inside.

"Well I can say this has certainly been the most memorable week of my life, and it hasn't been the easiest week of my life, but there is nobody I would rather spend it with then you," Ethan said as he toasted to Marissa as all of the women at the table began clapping.

"It's getting pretty close to midnight, do you think we should go out on the beach so that we can see the fireworks when the New Year rolls over," Denise said.

"I don't know, maybe it would be better for us if we all just stayed inside," Marissa said looking over at Ethan, and seeing that he was clearly uncomfortable still at the idea of going outside naked on the beach where everybody could see him.

Ethan shook his head. "No, I don't want you to bring in the New Year stuck in some type of cabin when we could be on the beach with fireworks and everything."

"But Ethan I want to ring in the new year with you," Marissa said.

"And that we will, outside on the beach," Ethan said with a smile as Marissa kissed him.

"Really you mean it, you're willing to go out naked completely on the beach like that for me?"

"I would go anywhere with you, clothing not required!"

Marissa was practically giddy as she was jumping up and down and preparing to go out on the beach.

"Aren't you coming Ethan?" Marissa said suddenly feeling that maybe he had gotten cold feet at the last moment after all of that.

"You go ahead, I will catch up with you in just a few minutes, I just have to do something," Ethan said as he went into the other room and opened up his suitcase where he kept the diamond ring. He opened up the case and saw that it was still in there, glistening brightly, and that is when he took the ring out and clenched it tightly in his left hand.

"Well it's now or never I suppose," Ethan said as he started walking out on to the beach where he saw Marissa and her girlfriends looking up and waiting for the fireworks.

"Well it looks like the New Year's going to be here any moment now, I guess you're getting excited that you're finally going to be able to put on your clothing again," Marissa said. "I don't blame you, as much as I have been enjoying all of this. You've been a really good sport Ethan, about everything, and I just can't express to you how proud I have been of you in the last few days. This has been the best vacation of my life for more reasons than one, and I hope that you feel the same way."

Ethan smiled and nodded. "It has certainly been the most memorable vacation of my life as well, and I couldn't think of anybody that I would have wanted to spend it with, clothed, dressed or otherwise than you. But Marissa right now I am not excited at the prospect of putting on my clothing, there's something else far more exciting and it goes along with what I was just saying about how there was nobody else in this world that I would rather spend my time with, or spend the rest of my life with." Ethan got down on one knee.

"Ethan what are you doing?" Marissa said as she saw him naked and vulnerable at her feet like that.

"Marissa Rogers, will you do me the pleasure of becoming my wife, in sickness and in health, in wealth or in poverty, wearing clothes or stuck eternally naked until death do us part for as long as we shall live?" Ethan said as he opened his hand and held out the diamond ring and put it on her finger.

Marissa wiped away a tear. "Yes, a million times yes!"

Ethan stood up and hugged and kissed her and began spinning her around in the air as people started counting down from 10 until the fireworks went off and everybody started shouting happy New Year.

"The perfect beginning to a new year, and the perfect beginning to the rest of our lives," Ethan said as they kissed again and watched the fireworks signifying that the New Year had rolled over.

All of Marissa's girlfriends started congratulating her and Ethan, and that was when they saw somebody that they did not want to see coming their way.

"Well well well, what is everybody over here so happy about," Tricia said as she walked over with her hands on her hips.

Marissa got right up in Tricia's face. "Listen bitch, nobody is going to ruin my man's New Year's, and it is most certainly not going to be you. This is the night of my engagement and I just like to say that you lose, I win," Marissa said as she showed her diamond ring.

"Well well well, I'm wondering where he was hiding that," Tricia said as she laughed. But as Marissa stood there with Ethan naked at her side, and all of her girlfriends staring down Tricia, Tricia realized what the score was and slowly started backing off before turning and walking away.

As they stood on the beach cheering and celebrating as Tricia walked off in shame, Ethan had never felt better. Once the fireworks and other festivities had died down they made their way back to the cabin and in through the door.

"Well Ethan I suppose we know what you want to do right now," Marissa said. "It's after midnight; I suppose this is the moment of truth, whether to see whether your wish has come true."

Ethan looked at Marissa and smiled. "You said yes, my most important wish has come true, everything else can wait."

The two of them stood there smiling, Marissa with her new engagement ring glistening on her finger, as she led Ethan into the bedroom, pushed him down and let him know that regardless of what happened when he went to get dressed in the morning just to it was who was wearing the pants in this relationship, and about that they were both very happy.

Epilogue

"I am so proud of you Ethan, as you didn't even mind going through the x-ray devices for security," Marissa said as they began boarding their plane.

"Well I figure at least anybody who happens to be looking is only seeing my skeleton," Ethan said as he laughed. "Besides after they vacation that we have been through, let's just say it changes a guy."

"It's ironic that after having such a wonderful vacation that we are so exhausted that we are probably going to need a vacation just to recover from our vacation," Marissa said.

"But I think that that's the way of knowing that it was a successful vacation, any vacation worth its salt is pretty much one that you need a vacation from when you get back because it was just so damn exciting. I don't know if it was all just psychosomatic or whether it really was magic, but every moment with you is magical as far as I am concerned. Just the same I'll just be glad that we can maybe relax and put all of this behind us and begin planning our new life together."

"You mean you're not worried that the plane is going to be attacked by gremlins or deadly snakes?"

"Marissa after everything that I experienced this week I have realized that there is nothing in this world scarier than being naked in public, after that I think that if we do find some snakes or gremlins on a plane that it would be quite easy to deal with by comparison, so I say bring them on!"

The two of them got on their plane and Ethan had to admit that after everything he had been through he wasn't even shy about using the bathroom anymore, which Marissa had to admit was a little bit disappointing, seeing as she enjoyed seeing him all anxious and squirming in his seat to use the bathroom, but she figured she had plenty of that in the future now that they were going to be together.

Later that night as they were looking out the window Ethan smiled as he could see some meteors shooting through the sky.

"Why are you smiling?" Marissa asked.

"Nothing, I just see some shooting stars, and seeing as you have had luck in the past, well weddings are expensive and everything, I guess what I am saying is do you think that you could perhaps wish that we win the lottery?"

Marissa laughed and pushed him playfully in the arm. "I am pretty sure that the chances of something like that happening again are pretty slim, I think that we probably only get one wish per customer don't you think?"

Ethan nodded. "Maybe I should be the one to make the wish this time, even though my wish of marrying you has already come true, that was not one that I wished for on a shooting star, that was just do to me being the luckiest guy in the world."

Marissa kissed him on the cheek as Ethan looked out the window, closed his eyes and decided to make a wish on a shooting star.

Marissa sat back in the airplane seat and that was when she started scratching herself all over.

"Ethan what did you wish for?" Marissa said as the two of them began laughing nervously.

Ethan simply shook his head and continued laughing. All he

could think to himself was that at least Marissa was the one who was the natural exhibitionist, because he didn't want to tell her how long he had made his wish for, as it was a whole lot longer than a single week!

Bonus Stories
My Night as a Naked Secret Santa

"I can't believe that this was totally okayed," Scott said.

"Well it was," Mike said. "The office said that as long as the women were comfortable with it there could be something like a naked secret Santa, and the response from the women was an overwhelming sense of excitement and enthusiasm. Besides it's going to be completely anonymous, so whoever ends up being selected to be the naked secret Santa will be wearing a Santa Claus beard and hat, so nobody will know who the naked guy is."

"I think they can make an educated guess," Scott said shaking his head.

"Well you don't have to participate in it if you don't want to, but all of the guys thought that it would be kind of a fun thing to do for all of the ladies."

"Yeah but only one guy is going to end up having to strip naked for every woman in the office! And there are a lot more women in this office then there are men."

"But there are 15 guys in the office, the way I see it you only have one in 15 chance of being picked as the naked secret Santa. But if you don't want to do it no one's going to force you to do it if you are uncomfortable with it. We just thought it would be sort of a nice thing to do for all of the women, and they all seemed really excited about it."

"So what exactly does the naked secret Santa have to do?"

"Well essentially you would just distribute all of the other secret Santa gifts to all of the women; you know but doing it completely buck naked in a Santa Claus beard and red Santa hat, you know to preserve the secret part of it."

"But I still think that the women might manage to figure it out somehow."

"Well you are not going to talk the whole time, that's the entire point. By wearing the beard and the hat and not saying anything nobody will know for sure who it is. I am sure that people will probably speculate, but as long as you have that beard and hat on no one's ever going to know for sure."

"Okay fine I will do it; I want to be a good sport and don't want to let the women down, since it's nice to do something for women around Christmas time. Besides the odds are it will be somebody else anyway."

Later at the end of the day.

"And our naked secret Santa is," Mike said looking at Scott trying hard not to smirk.

"Seriously?" Scott said. "I feel that this whole thing was rigged."

"But we just put names in a hat, it wasn't like we voted on who was going to be the secret Santa," Mike said. "But I guess if you don't want to be a team player and do it –"

"I'll do it, I'll do it," Scott said waving his hands. "I'm just saying that the odds of this happening, why am I just not surprised?"

Mike smiled. "Hey I would do it, but I wasn't the one who got picked and everything like that." Mike smiled as he held up the Santa beard and hat. "So do you want to get dressed in your costume now?"

"It looks a bit drafty," Scott said, but now he couldn't help but laugh. It was kind of funny he had to admit, and at least the ladies would get a thrill out of it, it wasn't like they would ever know it was him.

Scott quickly went behind the curtain and got changed into his costume and all of the guys couldn't help but snicker and laugh.

"Hey Santa I can see your sack," Mike said as he burst out laughing and pointed at Scott's genitals.

"I've got my sack right here," Scott said as he threw the sack full of presents over his shoulder. As he was standing there naked wearing a Santa Claus beard attached to a hat with a little ball on the end of it and carrying a huge sack full of presents over his shoulder, he had to admit that he had never felt more ridiculous in his entire life.

"Well Santa get your naked ass out there into the office and start distributing those gifts," Mike said as he laughed and pointed at Scott who simply shook his head and slowly approached the door to the office. "What's the matter, getting cold feet?"

"My feet aren't the only thing that's cold right now," Scott said realizing that he probably had obvious goosebumps from the cold. He continued to hesitate before he took a deep breath, sucked it up, opened the door and walked out into the office to see about two dozen women all screaming and clapping.

"Yea, Santa is here, are we on the naughty list Santa?" Claire said as she began whistling and hollering. Scott had to admit that he always had a real major crush on Claire, and he couldn't help but feel nervous at the thought that maybe she realized it was him.

"Ho Ho Ho," Scott muttered before coughing into his fist remembering that he wasn't supposed to say anything and that he didn't want to give away his identity.

"Well it looks like Santa is happy to see us," Marissa said as she pointed at Scott who suddenly realized that to his great humiliation this whole experience had given him a huge throbbing erection that was pointed right at her.

"This is the best Christmas ever," Karen said as she started laughing. "Maybe Santa will let us sit on his lap!"

"If Santa Claus has room in his lap with that thing dangling off of it," Deborah said, as she couldn't help but giggle and point.

Scott suddenly found himself paralyzed with fear, as he had never found himself more humiliated. But then he thought to himself that he was completely anonymous, that was the secret part of secret Santa. None of these women had any idea that it was him, how could they?

As soon as he realized that there was no way they could ever confirm with 100% certainty that it was him he suddenly started relaxing a little bit, his erection even subsided a little bit, at least until Claire bent over giving him a good look at her cleavage.

Once again taking a deep breath, Scott simply went around quietly distributing the gifts to the women, who all smiled and struggled to repress the urge to burst out laughing as a naked Santa Claus went around handing them each gifts from his sack until it was basically empty. That was when he realized that he only had one present left and started looking around to see if there was anyone who hadn't gotten one yet.

"Hey Santa Claus I haven't gotten any yet," Claire said as she waved to him with a huge smile on her face.

As Scott stood there directly in line with Claire, he once again became instantaneously erect and found his heart pounding out of his chest with excitement. He felt almost paralyzed again, like he could barely move. He reached into his sack and pulled out the last gift and slowly started walking towards Claire, his legs now shaking as much with fear as with excitement.

He had almost made his way across the room holding the gift in his hand, when all of a sudden his hands started shaking and he dropped it and it fell to the floor with a thud. Now he felt extremely awkward because not only was he a naked Santa, he was a clumsy naked Santa, and he had dropped the gift right in front of the woman that he had the hugest crush on.

Not sure exactly what to do, he slowly started reaching down to pick up the gift as he heard women whistling and shouting nice ass, when he then noticed that Claire was also likewise reaching towards the present. As he was coming up he felt his hat, which was attached to his beard, hit Claire underneath her chin causing it to fall right off.

Scott froze as he realized that now he was completely uncovered. Strangely enough he never felt completely naked as long as he had that beard and hat on, even though the ladies could see all of the interesting parts of his anatomy, but now his identity was exposed, exposed for every single woman in the office to see. He would never be able to live this down. He would have to leave the office forever and find a new job, and he was just starting to really like it there a lot.

As he stood there holding up the gift and pushing it towards Claire, she took it from his hands, slowly bent down, picked up his hat and beard and put it back on his face as she walked away, smiled and winked at him.

He couldn't believe it; Claire had just saved his life. Sure she knew he was Santa Claus, but none of the other women in the office had seen his face because he had his back to them, all they saw was his ass!

Very slowly Scott turned around and faced all of the other women who started clapping and cheering and whistling once more. Scott simply waved to them, picked up his empty sack and hightailed it out of there as all of the women started going crazy with excitement.

"Well it sounds like you got a pretty big standing ovation," Mike said as he closed the door behind him. "So how was it?"

Scott started to feel wobbly and that was when he fell down on the floor and passed out.

Mike shook his head as he looked at the other guys. "I am not homophobic or anything but if you think I'm going to perform mouth-to-mouth on a naked Santa Claus you've got another thing coming!"

Scott soon recovered from his total state of shock, quickly got dressed and was eager to get home. He knew that night was the most humiliating night of his life, and yet he had never been horny like he had been at that moment. He started masturbating furiously and instantaneously blew his load and then finally managed to get to sleep.

He had no idea how he was going to face Claire at the office when they got back from Christmas break. But when he got back from Christmas, the first day back, he saw a little tiny present on his desk. It didn't seem to have any name on it or anything like that, and he didn't see who left it there. He couldn't find Claire anywhere in the office and he was wondering if she felt as awkward about having seen him as he being seen by her, if anything like that were even possible. He was hoping that she didn't quit just because of the whole awkwardness of the situation. Why on earth had he ever agreed to be a naked secret Santa?

Looking around at the women in the office he couldn't see any obvious signs that any of the other women in the office knew that it was him. The women looked over at him occasionally, but they looked at the other guys as well. He was wondering if they were all sizing the guys up and trying to guess who the naked secret Santa was. But that's when it dawned on him, Claire had never given away his identity, she must have kept his secret.

"God bless her," Scott said as he opened up the little package which simply had a small note in it. "Meet me at the following location at lunch time if you want a Christmas gift you will never forget."

Scott wasn't sure how to regard this present, and he was getting nervous as lunch approached. But as soon as lunch approached he went down to the location written on the card and opened the door and closed it behind him. He found himself in a dark room and he felt around for the light switch until he turned it on, at which point he saw that standing there naked, wearing nothing but the same hat that he had been wearing, minus the beard, was Claire with a big smile on her face.

"Do you like your Christmas gift Santa Claus?" Claire said as she stood there laughing as she looked right between his legs. "Well it seems like once again you are happy to see me, I know that much!"

Scott wasn't exactly sure how to respond to such an unprecedented turn of events other than to smile. "Well Claire, this is certainly a side of you I have never seen before."

"What about this side," she said as she turned around and shook her naked ass at him as she smacked it with her hands before she burst out laughing.

"I think that you look pretty good from any angle," Scott said as she turned back around and he could tell that she was blushing but still smiling all the while. "But isn't it a little bit late for a Christmas gift?"

Claire shook her head. "Well if you don't want it I'm afraid that you can't exchange it!"

The two of them burst out laughing as Scott looked at her directly in the eyes with a big smile on his face. "You know I wouldn't even think of it. Merry Christmas Claire!"

"Merry Christmas St. Nick, and a very happy new year!"

And as Scott approached the naked love of his life, standing there in front of him, he realized that it was not going to be a good new year, it was going to be the greatest new year of his life.

<u>Our Holiday as Naked Christmas Trees</u>

"I really do need some type of job for the holidays," Sabrina said to herself shaking her head. She knew that there was no way she would be able to afford any type of Christmas presents for her friends and family now that she had lost her job just around the holiday season.

"How about this, all you have to do is be a Christmas tree," said her friend Hillary as she pointed to an ad in the paper.

"How on earth does somebody be a Christmas tree?"

Hillary shook her head. "I honestly don't know, but they are paying $2000 for a single night of it, so whatever it involves to be a Christmas tree it sounds like it's a very lucrative job offer. Come to think of it for $2000 I could be a Christmas tree for one night, why not?"

Sabrina looked at the ad and shook her head. "Look I'm sure that if they are paying us $2000 to be a Christmas tree this probably some type of terrible catch. And why is the job only available to women?"

"I don't know if there is a terrible catch but whatever it is for $2000 it's probably worth it, I say that we should check it out."

"I guess it can't hurt to try," Sabrina said and the two of them called to set up a job interview for being a Christmas tree.

"I should admit right off the bat that neither of us has any experience being a Christmas tree," Sabrina said as they sat down at the place to be interviewed.

The interviewer looked them both over and smiled. "Well you are both very attractive women, so I think that you will make perfect Christmas trees."

"So you are saying that we got the job?" Hillary asked.

"Yeah, the people we're holding the Christmas party for love blondes and redheads, so I think that you will make excellent Christmas trees," the interviewer said as they shook their heads. "I will give you the address and you just report for work and we will tell you everything that you need to do to be the perfect Christmas tree."

"Well that was certainly easy," Hillary said as they walked out of the office. "All they did was take a look at us and they said that we were the perfect Christmas trees. Although given that I have no idea what being a Christmas tree entails I don't know if that should be taken as a compliment or some type of insult."

"You mean like when people say that I am a dumb blonde," Sabrina said. "Like you are the perfect Christmas tree, because a Christmas tree just stands there like an idiot and doesn't do anything, because I do kind of feel that this sounds like a weird job, I mean it couldn't be a very intellectually demanding job to be a Christmas tree I am guessing. The fact that they just gave us the job based on our looks alone should raise a red flag, but I suppose if it's just posing as a Christmas tree there's nothing bad about that. For $2000

I can spend one night standing around dressed up like a Christmas tree."

"You think it's going to be some type of weird costume where we have to wear a costume like some type of Christmas tree costume or something?"

"I have just as little experience being a Christmas tree as you do, we will find out when we get there. But for $2000 I am sure that whatever it is they are probably paying us excessively for what should probably be easy work."

That Christmas Eve the two of them arrived at the address that they were given. They went into an area where they saw a whole bunch of other women, all of whom looked rather attractive they thought, lined up and smiling.

"Are you here for the Christmas tree job?" a man said as he came over to them.

The two of them nodded and he directed them to line up with all the other women. That was when a man came out dressed as Santa Claus.

"Excellent, you all look like you will make excellent Christmas trees," the man dressed as Santa Claus said. "My name is Karl Meriwether the third and I am your wealthy host this evening. You have all been selected because you have been deemed worthy of being Christmas trees at our party. Now if you'll come back with me we will get you into your Christmas costumes."

Sabrina and Hillary looked at each other and shrugged their shoulders as they followed Karl to the back area along with all of the other women.

The man dressed as Santa Claus, otherwise known as Karl, looked them over and smiled. "Well we have a great selection of Christmas trees this year, so I want you to all get undressed and we will give you your costumes."

Sabrina raised her hand and Karl pointed at her. "You want us to just get undressed right here in the lobby? You don't want us to maybe go to a dressing room?"

Karl laughed. "Well if you are shy you certainly have picked the wrong job deciding to be a Christmas tree."

Hillary raised her hand. "Didn't you say that we would be getting costumes?"

Karl nodded. "As soon as you are all completely undressed we will give you your Christmas tree costumes."

"So you are saying you want us all to just get completely buck naked right now?" Sabrina said shaking her head. "I knew there would probably be some terrible catch to this job."

Karl shook his head. "Like I said if you are shy this is not the job for you, so if you don't want to get naked I suggest that you leave and we will have to find somebody else who would be more willing to do your job."

Sabrina was about to leave when Hillary grabbed her by the arm. "Did you forget that we already spent a whole lot of money on our credit cards, and if we don't get this job we won't be able to pay off our credit card debt anytime in the next decade?"

Sabrina shook her head. "I am not going to get completely naked in the middle of a lobby where this strange guy dressed as Santa Claus is telling me to get undressed."

"Don't worry, they said that they are going to give us costumes, I'm sure that they don't expect us to be standing around naked all evening, that would just be absurd."

"I think that we should have expected the absurd when we responded to an ad asking for people who wanted to be Christmas trees. But as much as I hate to admit it you are right, I have already bought tons of Christmas presents that I can't really return based on the fact that I was expecting the $2000 for this job to pay it off. I guess I will just have to hope the costume is not too revealing."

"Ladies I don't see you getting undressed," Karl said as he came by in his Santa Claus outfit and patted his stomach.

Sabrina and Hillary looked at each other and very awkwardly and very slowly got undressed until they were standing there naked with a line of about two dozen other naked women. Hillary and Sabrina had never seen each other naked outside of a locker room before, and they felt weird to be standing there naked in the lobby together and were unconsciously trying to cover themselves up, as they could see that other women in the lobby looked like they were shivering and getting goosebumps as well.

"So are you going to give us our costumes right now?" Sabrina said.

"In just a moment," Karl said as he clapped his hands and a bunch of men in tuxedos came out and started handing out angel hats with stars on top, a bunch of Christmas lights and two little ornaments shaped like balls.

"What the hell is all of this?" Sabrina said.

Karl laughed. "I can see that you have never been a Christmas tree before! Those are your outfits. The angel hat goes on your head, the Christmas lights you wrap around your body, and those two little Christmas ornaments will hang off of your nipples!"

"That's not a costume, that's pretty much the same as being naked!" Sabrina shouted.

Karl laughed. "Exactly, you are going to be a naked Christmas tree. This is a party for lots of wealthy men who like to celebrate Christmas each year by seeing lots of hot naked women dressed up in a Christmasy way, but still basically undressed."

"This is just blatant objectification," Sabrina said. "Literally you are turning us into naked objects for everybody to gawk at."

Karl smiled. "Do you have a point that you are trying to make?"

"There is no way I'm going to stand here on display all night as a naked Christmas tree!" Sabrina said as she was about to march away when Hillary grabbed her. "What is it Hillary?"

"$2000 in credit card debt you will never otherwise pay off anytime soon," Hillary said as Sabrina cringed and stood there and grabbed her costume.

"Excellent, I'm glad you came around to our point of view," Karl said. "You are going to make this a very Merry Christmas for lots of rich horny men, you should be proud!"

Sabrina cringed as she looked at her costume but reluctantly put the angel hat on her head, which had a glowing star on the top of the angel, wrapped herself in Christmas tree lights and hung the Christmas tree ornaments off of her nipples.

"So how do I look?" Hillary said as she stood there in her costume completely naked except for a bunch of Christmas tree accessories that didn't really hide anything at all.

"You look almost as ridiculous as I do, these costumes leave basically nothing whatsoever to the imagination. Can you just promise me one thing?"

"What's that?"

"When this night is over I never want this to be mentioned again, ever. In fact never even mention Christmas trees to me again.

Just the mention of Christmas trees is going to remind me of this!"

Hillary laughed. "I see your point."

"I don't know how you could possibly be laughing at this!"

Hillary shrugged her shoulders. "I mean this is embarrassing as hell, but what are you going to do? For $2000 I'm willing to stand around naked covered in Christmas tree lights for a few hours. I think you just have to laugh at the absurdity of the situation."

Sabrina shook her head. "The thing that annoys me is that we are basically just high paid sexual decorations for a bunch of horny rich jerks who could buy and sell our asses, or in this case stare at them, and who basically can just use their privilege to get us to do this."

"Yeah, for like $2000, that's not bad!" Hillary said as she nodded and smiled.

"I guess that I am the idealist but even I can't afford my own dignity now, so let's just get this over with and hopefully the time will pass by quickly."

Karl instructed all of the women to space out a little bit and stand around in the lobby as they waited for the partiers to arrive. Sabrina had to admit that she never had felt more absurd in her entire life, and she felt really self-conscious standing there naked with all of these other naked women covered in Christmas tree lights and ornaments.

"Okay ladies the party is about to begin!" Karl said as he opened the door and a bunch of men in tuxedos came in and started clapping.

"Well this is a Merry Christmas!" the man at the head of the group of men said. "These are the loveliest naked Christmas trees I have ever seen before. Look how lovely they are decorated."

That was when Sabrina could practically just die right then and there, because that was when she noticed who the man was, it was Philip Carson, the rich jerk that was always hitting on her in high school and was just a snobby stuck up asshole in general. He couldn't understand why anyone wouldn't want to go out with a rich person like he was despite his total lack of redeeming qualities, and he always resented Sabrina for turning down his advances. She just hoped to God that by all that was holy that he wouldn't notice who she was.

"Oh God," Sabrina said as Hillary looked at her.

"What is it?" Hillary whispered to her from a few feet away.

"Don't you recognize who that is," Sabrina said as Philip walked over and smiled at her. That was when she decided that she would shut up before she made herself stand out in the crowd.

"Well well well, this Christmas tree certainly has a mouth on her doesn't it," Philip said as he walked over to Sabrina. "What were you whispering about to your fellow Christmas tree? You look kind of familiar, have I seen you before?"

"Not like this you haven't," Sabrina said before covering up her mouth.

Philip smiled. "Well well well, if it isn't Sabrina, I thought you looked familiar somewhere, I didn't recognize you at first because I guess I haven't seen you dressed, or rather undressed like this before. I have to say it's a really good look on you and I will enjoy watching you this evening. In fact I think I'm going to spend my entire evening admiring the foliage over here." Philip looked down between Sabrina's legs at her unshaven pubic hair which caused her to unconsciously press her legs together, but she couldn't hide anything from him.

Sabrina knew that by now she was blushing bright red and she was practically shaking at the knees, but she didn't want to make it look like he was getting to her, so she stood there and said nothing.

"That is good, good Christmas trees are meant to be seen and not heard," Philip said. "Let the festivities begin!"

Sabrina gritted her teeth as man after man came over by her and took their pictures with her as she just stood there trying not to say or do anything and trying to picture that she was somewhere else, fully dressed and not buck naked at a Christmas party for a bunch of drunken rich idiots.

Hillary could see that this was just completely destroying Sabrina. She wanted to say something but she wasn't the type to speak up in situations like this, which was usually Sabrina, but now to see Sabrina silenced like that was frightening to Hillary. She could see that Sabrina was paralyzed with complete and utter humiliation to the point where she literally was frozen in place.

"But everybody this is my favorite Christmas tree right here," Philip said as he drank some eggnog and pointed at Sabrina. He was clearly drunk. "Just look at how perfect it is, look at every little inch of it, every little inch finally on display. You have no idea how many years I wanted to unwrap this present, and now here she is, completely unwrapped and on display. But you know I think that we could unwrap her further, what do you say guys?"

All of the guys started hooting and hollering as Philip took off the hat, took off the ornaments and took off the lights until Sabrina was now completely uncovered and still standing there still as still as a statue. Philip paced back and forth all around her looking at every inch of her body and feeling it with his hands as she just stood there trying to prevent her lip from trembling.

"Well well well, all Christmas trees are naked, but it seems some Christmas trees are more naked than others," Philip said as all the guys began laughing. "You know it really is good to be rich like this, every Christmas is a Merry Christmas, but this has to be the best Christmas of all. There is absolutely nothing that could ruin this moment for me. My silent naked little Christmas tree, I have finally gotten to unwrap you at last, and you have nothing to say about it."

Sabrina had now felt like she had entered another reality altogether. She knew that if she said or did anything that she would probably be expelled and wouldn't get her pay and would never be able to pay off her credit card debt. So she just fought against every fiber of her being and continued to stand there, fighting back tears as Philip continued to feel up her body.

As all of the men stood there staring at Sabrina on display that was when they started hearing something. Standing next to Sabrina was Hillary taking off her Christmas lights, her angel hat and her nipple ornaments until she was standing there completely naked, standing right next to Sabrina, and looked contemptuously at Philip and turned her head away in disgust.

Soon all of the other women in the room started taking off their lights, their hats and their ornaments until they were all completely stark naked with no cover whatsoever, and they all started to gather around Sabrina until they had blocked her from view completely.

"What is this, some type of a rebellion?" Philip asked, realizing he was losing face with the other men who were just sort of standing there nervously and looking uncomfortable, perhaps even more uncomfortable than the two dozen naked women surrounding Sabrina at that moment. "You realize that if you go against the rules we don't have to pay you."

The other men started to back off as the naked women looked angry and started gathering around Philip until he was completely surrounded.

"What is the meaning of this?" Philip said as all of the women dove on top of him and started tearing his clothes off until he was now completely naked in the middle of the room as all of the naked woman stood around him smiling as Philip's tiny penis began to become erect.

"Well it seems one of us seems to be a little bit more turned on by naked humiliation than others," Hillary finally said as all of the women began laughing. Then soon all of the men in the audience started clapping and laughing as well.

Philip stormed angrily outside of the room as he gathered up his clothing to the sound of dozens of camera phones going off, and began cursing and shouting about how the party was now over and that everyone should go home.

As Philip left the room all of the guys turned to the crowd of naked women with Sabrina standing in the center still not saying anything and looking as though she was in a trancelike state, a state of total shock. Then surprisingly all of the men began clapping and cheering.

The women stood there naked for a while but then started getting dressed as the partygoers started slowly leaving one by one until it was finally okay for all of the women to get dressed. Hillary helped Sabrina to get dressed but the entire time she did so Sabrina hadn't said a single thing.

"Hey are you okay?" Hillary said as she waved her hand in front of a now dressed Sabrina.

"Thank you," Sabrina said after a long pause.

"For what?"

"For speaking up when I was too paralyzed with fear to speak up for once. You were the one who really managed to keep your dignity; you are the real idealist, not me. I always shout about these things but as soon as I was standing there naked I just completely froze, became paralyzed with fear."

Hillary patted her on the back. "Hey it's okay, we all get really embarrassed sometime, and in fact I don't see how you could not get embarrassed in a situation like that. Believe me I know that I was sure embarrassed and I know that a lot of the other women in there were embarrassed as well. But hey sometimes you have to do what you have to do. Do you think they will still pay us?"

Sabrina shook her head. "I have no idea, and I don't even care now. I am just glad to be out of there. But at least Philip got his comeuppance."

"I know, and did you see his teeny tiny little baby penis," Hillary said as she squeezed her fingers together and put a circle around her eye like she was looking at them with a magnifying glass as the two of them burst into laughter.

The two of them then laughed the entire way home.

Unfortunately Philip, having suffered the humiliation of his life, wasn't about to pay those women who rebelled against him at his own party, and Sabrina had no idea how she was going to pay off her credit card debt, until one day she was invited to a special event.

"But what is this all about?" Sabrina asked as she walked into a room where a bunch of men and women all jumped out and shouted surprise.

"You have no idea what this is about do you?" Hillary said as Sabrina shook her head. "Well after what happened that whole incident with Philip went viral and it turns out there were a lot of people who liked to see a rich jerk like him get his comeuppance. In fact some of his friends from the party admired what we did so much that they felt bad and they decided to chip in some money as well. We started a go fund me page for you, and long story short you might have to stop constantly putting down all of those rich assholes."

"What are you talking about?" Sabrina said still not exactly sure what was going on.

Hillary took out her phone and brought up a go fund me page and showed it to Sabrina. "Let's just say I don't think you're ever going to have to worry about being in credit card debt ever again, and that I think you're going to have a very very happy new year."

Sabrina's eyes were bugging out of her head as she looked at the device. "Is that really the correct number of zeros?"

Hillary nodded as Sabrina started to grow faint, but before she fainted a guy caught her and she couldn't help but notice him from the party, a really attractive guy that she had been looking at and was especially embarrassed to be found naked in front of.

"Hey, you don't know me but I am Mark, and I always thought that Philip was a jerk, and I felt really bad what he did about you. And I hope that you're not going to take this the wrong way or anything, but you were definitely the most attractive Christmas tree at the party."

"Hey what about me," Hillary said as she put her hands on her hips and then began laughing.

"I was just wondering if you don't think I'm just some type of rich jerk, the type who goes to parties like that, well I would really like to go out with you sometime, whatever you want to wear being fine with me," Mark said as he laughed.

Sabrina laughed and kissed him before blushing again when she realized that he had already seen her naked. That was when she smiled deviously and whispered in his ear causing him to blush as she then walked away, but not before throwing her coat over an exposed Christmas tree that was on the floor next to her and laughing.

"What did she tell you?" Hillary said. "Whatever it is it made you blush!"

Mark laughed. "She said that she would love to go out on a date with me, but then when we did it was my turn to be the Christmas tree!"

<u>Naked Underneath the Mistletoe</u>

"I was wondering if you wanted to go to the Christmas party, you know just as friends or something like that," Chris said nervously asking Laura if she wanted to go to the Christmas party at Jerome's house.

"Just as friends then," Laura said, almost as equally as awkward as Chris about the whole idea of going to a Christmas party together. "But isn't that the really crazy Christmas party where things get really out of hand, as I've heard that the things there can get pretty wild and kind of crazy and everything like that."

"I've heard that he has a reputation for craziness too, but I mean we don't have to participate in the craziness, I'm sure we could just go and have a fun time at the party, and we don't have to play any drinking games or do any drugs or anything that's going to be too off-the-wall."

"Well I guess we could go to the Christmas party, again just as friends and everything like that, I'm sure it will be fun, and I guess we all have to let loose sometimes right?"

"Yeah we have to live a little," Chris said laughing as they agreed to meet that Saturday to go to the party together.

That Saturday Chris arrived to pick up Laura really early so that they could get to the party on time, but he had to admit that while they were driving to the party he was finding it awkward to make conversation, he was never very good at small talk. Laura was really attractive and everything like that and he found that intimidating, but he didn't realize that Laura was really attracted to him but was hoping that he would be one to make a move.

"Well here we are at the party," Chris said as he pulled up in front of the house to realize that there were tons of cars up and down the street, so it was amazing that they were able to get a parking spot up front like that.

"Well it looks a lot more crowded than I ever thought, I mean I heard that he often had a big blowout and everything like that but there are probably dozens of people at this party. I hope things don't get too wild and out of hand."

"How crazy could things possibly get at one little party like this? I am sure that we are probably just blowing it out of proportion, you'll see, it's just going to be a normal ordinary party and I'm sure that nothing weird is going to go on."

Laura nodded. "You are right, we should stop being so uptight and just learn to unwind and live and let live and enjoy the party."

They rang the doorbell and Jerome opened the door not recognizing them right away. "Chris and Laura right," he said eventually as the two of them nodded. "Well make yourself comfortable and enjoy the party."

As Chris and Laura got into the main room of the house and saw that everybody looked like they were in a festive mood they began to relax a little. It didn't seem like people were snorting cocaine off of the blade of a knife or doing anything else really ludicrous, it looked like everyone just enjoying a normal party. A couple of people were drinking but there was nothing wrong with that as they were sure that it probably wouldn't get out of hand.

"Chris and Laura, so nice of you to make it, I was hoping you guys would show up," Edith said as she came by with her husband Jack. "Are the two of you a couple now?"

"No!" they both said looking at each other awkwardly before looking down at their feet.

"We just came as friends and everything like that," Chris said, seemingly blushing at the idea that they were immediately pegged as a couple just because they had arrived together.

"Well I'm glad to see that you have found a way to unwind and decided to come to the party, you know these parties can get kind of crazy," Jack said as he laughed.

"So we've heard, but it looks pretty ordinary right now," Laura said.

Jack laughed. "Well we have some crazy party games later on, and there are a whole bunch of rules about the party that if you have never been here before you might not be aware of, so be on the lookout."

As Jack and Edith went off Chris and Laura looked at each other somewhat nervously.

"What do you think he meant by that?" Laura said as Chris shrugged his shoulders.

"I have no idea, but I'm sure that we are not going to break any type of rules," Chris said and the two of them began mingling around and talking with friends.

"So you really got Laura to come to the party with you, that's pretty cool, she's a real hot lady," Chris's friend Erik said.

"Yeah I'm impressed that you got her to come with you," Ryan said.

"We are just here as friends," Chris said as they all sort of looked at each other rolling their eyes.

"Right you keep telling yourself that buddy," Erik said as he patted Chris on the back and began walking off.

Chris had to admit he still felt rather awkward around Laura and wasn't exactly sure how to make a move, as he wasn't really good at these type of social affairs. He figured that he had better go see Laura so that it didn't seem like they were avoiding one another.

Laura was talking to a bunch of her friends as Chris came over with a smile on his face.

"And here's Chris, we're here, well we just came here as

friends," Laura said once again sort of awkwardly fiddling with her thumbs.

"Oh my God!" Laura's girlfriend Rebecca shouted as she pointed to the two of them. "Mistletoe, they're underneath the mistletoe!"

All of the other women began shouting and pointing at them shouting the word mistletoe over and over again as all of the sudden a light shined on them.

This is exactly what they didn't want, they didn't want to draw attention to themselves, and now they found a spotlight on them.

"Well well well, it looks like the first couple to go under the mistletoe tonight, you know what that means," Jerome said as everybody began laughing.

Chris found his heart racing, did they really expect him to kiss Laura underneath the mistletoe in front of everybody. They were just supposed to be there as friends, and he wasn't sure what the protocol was for a situation like this.

"Yeah we are just kind of friends," Chris said sort of awkwardly smiling at Laura who sort of awkwardly smiled back. "It feels kind of weird to kiss when we aren't even technically on a date."

Everyone in the audience began laughing and Chris felt like an idiot, here he was underneath the spotlight underneath the mistletoe with everybody expecting him to kiss Laura and he wasn't even going to do it, maybe he was a coward. Then he thought that he was being kind of silly, so he leaned forward and began approaching Laura to kiss her hoping that she wouldn't find the whole affair too awkward.

"Kiss, you thought that we expected you guys to kiss each other?" Jerome said as everybody burst out laughing.

"Isn't that what you do under the mistletoe," Chris said.

"Maybe at one of those high school parties or a normal Christmas party, but this isn't any ordinary Christmas party, this is the craziest Christmas party on the planet!" Jerome shouted as everybody began clapping. "I feel like you two didn't read the rules, so maybe somebody should remind you about what the rules are about the first people to be under the mistletoe tonight together."

"They have to get naked!" Miranda shouted as she whistled

with her fingers and everybody began clapping and cheering.

"Naked!" Chris and Laura said as they looked at each other before looking at everybody who was looking at them.

"Well that's a funny joke you guys," Chris said, laughing nervously.

But Chris realized this time nobody was laughing, and he started to get the distinct creepy feeling that they were actually serious.

"She's right you guys, the rules are that the first couple to get spotted under the mistletoe together have to get completely naked," Jerome said. "Those are rules and I am not about to start seeing my rules broken at my party, and rule breakers cannot stay at the party."

Chris thought this was ridiculous and was about to say something to that effect when Laura grabbed him by the arm and looked him in the eye with a penetrating glance of seriousness, and that was when he knew that she meant business.

"I think that we had better do what they say," Laura said, and Chris couldn't believe that she was actually saying that.

"So what do you guys say, are you going to play by the rules," Jerome said as all eyes were on them.

Chris was standing there nervous feeling like he was about to faint before he said the first stupid ass thing that came into his mouth. "Ladies first," he said as he looked at Laura and everybody began hooting and hollering.

At first he thought that what he did was really piggish of him, and he could see Laura making eye contact with him, glaring at him in an intimidating manner, before she shook her head and shrugged her shoulders.

"Hey I'm game," Laura said as she began undressing as everybody began clapping and cheering. Chris couldn't believe that Laura was actually doing that, as he always knew her to be especially bashful the way he was, and now here she was completely stripping down until she was standing there completely naked.

Chris's eyes practically bugged out of their sockets as he stood there seeing Laura looking incredibly uncomfortable being naked in front of a crowd who were looking at him waiting for him to make the next move. He swallowed deeply and slowly started getting undressed as people began clapping again.

"I'll take this, you'll get it back at the end of the night,"

Miranda said as she gathered up their clothing and put it in a Christmas bag that they decided to hang over the fireplace.

"Well I guess we should give our naked couple some space so that they can mingle with everybody," Jerome said as the two of them stood there awkwardly trying to cover themselves up.

For a long time neither of them said anything, but as everybody started turning away and minding their own business, Chris started walking over towards his friends who were pointing at him and laughing.

"You didn't read the rules did you," Jack said shaking his head as Chris came over.

"What kind of rule is it that you have to get naked if you are the first people under the mistletoe?!" Chris said.

"Rule number 12 I believe," Jack said as he looked at the list. "Nope it was number 13, lucky number 13!"

"Yeah real lucky," Chris said feeling like you wanted to go grab that bag and get out of there right now, except he didn't feel that would be fair to Laura who was bold enough to get naked first.

"What the hell dude, did you see the way that she was looking at you, you should be over there with Laura and her friends," Erik said shaking his head.

"Yeah we don't want to see your naked ass," Ryan said as Chris turned and looked across the room at Laura who was over there with her girlfriends who were all smirking and laughing and pointing at him and making him feel really self-conscious as he once again covered himself up.

"Dude don't be a pussy, go over there where all the women are, I think they really want to see you," Erik said as he laughed.

All of Laura's friends began laughing hysterically and trying to cover up their mouths because they were snickering as they saw Chris come over looking like an idiot with his hands over his crotch trying to cover himself up.

Laura's friends pushed her forward as she stood there in front of Chris, not exactly sure what to say as they were both blushing profusely and they realized that everyone was looking at them.

"So would you like to dance," Laura said as she swallowed deeply, struggling to make eye contact with Chris. "You know just as friends and everything."

Since when do friends dance together naked, Chris thought,

but as he saw Laura looking at him and smiling that was when he realized that whatever they were when they went to that party in the evening now they had certainly progressed past the friends stage, and right to the we are naked together in public phase, wherever that usually comes in the relationship.

As the two of them danced they couldn't help but burst out laughing.

"This really is the most ridiculous thing in the world," Chris said as Laura began laughing.

"The way I see it it's just two friends dancing together," Laura said, but she could see from looking between Chris's legs that he was a lot more happy to see her than he would someone who was just be a friend.

As the two of them continued dancing a crazy thing happened where it suddenly felt like everyone else in the room had gone away, like they were completely ignoring everybody else around them and just enjoying the moment. Of course when they realized that the spotlight was right on them again that was when they realized that they were most certainly not alone.

"Let's hear it for the naked mistletoe couple!" Jerome said as several people began clapping and Miranda began whistling and laughing her ass off.

As everybody was clapping and cheering for them, Chris simply took Laura by the hand and together they took a bow as the crowd went wild.

Then the craziest thing happened, where for the rest of the night they barely even thought about the fact that they were naked as they went around mingling and chatting with their friends. They couldn't go more than a few seconds without constantly looking at each other, stealing a glance before looking away before the other person realized what they were doing, but both of them realized obviously what they were doing.

The party lasted well into the night but finally the night was winding down.

"Well I'm really tempted to play keep away with this, but it is getting late," Miranda said as she handed them the bag containing their clothing and they got dressed.

"Thanks for coming you guys, you really were the life of the party," Jerome said as everybody said their goodbyes and Chris and

Laura went back out to the car.

"So that was some party wasn't it," Laura said as the two of them sat down.

"Yeah you're telling me, next time I think that we will have to read the rulebook when we go to a party like that," Chris said as they both laughed. "I just can't believe that we went along with all of that, and here we were saying we weren't going to go along with any of the craziness and let things get out of hand."

"Well I didn't think they really got out of hand, did you?" Laura said as Chris shrugged his shoulders.

The two of them sat there in awkward silence for a couple of moments before Chris figured that they had better be leaving. While they were at the party strangely enough it wasn't as awkward as it was now that they were together alone, both knowing that they had seen each other naked all night long, and that now they were just going home as though nothing had happened. Maybe they really were just still friends.

"Well here we are," Chris said as he pulled up in front of Laura's house. He knew he should say something more but he was finding himself tongue-tied on this particular occasion.

"Would you like to come in a minute," Laura said smiling in what he felt was a semi-devious way.

"Sure, I think I can at least walk you to the door," Chris said as the two of them got out of the car and got into Laura's doorway as they stood there smiling at each other. "Well it was a great night and everything."

"Chris aren't you forgetting something," Laura said as she pointed above them and that was when he noticed a mistletoe hanging over the doorway.

Chris leaned forward and kissed Laura as she smiled before laughing.

"What's so funny?" Chris asked feeling that he had done something stupid and made an idiot of himself.

"You are thinking of traditional mistletoe rules, I think that after tonight we know that there is a new rule about mistletoe," Laura said as she licked her lips and began pulling Chris inside the house.

And as Laura reached for the buttons of his shirt and began unbuttoning them he knew that this was definitely going to be the most Merry Christmas that he had ever had.

The Way God Made Us: The Story of the Naked Choir

"I don't know, are you sure you want to date Rebecca, she seems like one of those kinds of uptight women, and I heard that she is actually really religious and everything comes from an incredibly religious family," Jackson said.

"Okay so I'm not very religious," Ned said shaking his head. "I'm certainly no Ned Flanders, that's for sure. But look how damn hot Rebecca is, can you imagine being with a woman that attractive?"

"I wonder what she looks like naked!"

"Okay dude seriously you can't put that image in my head, because now I can't concentrate on anything else. But I don't care if she's religious, I could deal with that, I'm a little uptight myself, I'm not usually the type to get naked on a first date. It might be better to take it slow; being with sort of a shy conservative girl might actually not be so bad."

Jackson shook his head. "I don't know dude, if I was with a woman like that I would barely be able to restrain myself from tearing her clothing off at the first opportunity that she allowed. But I guess everybody's different."

"But I think I'm going to do it, I think that I am going to ask her out. I will have to just swallow my pride and try not to be so shy."

Ned went over to where Rebecca was and as soon as he saw her smiling at him he was already getting nervous and was thinking about turning around. The very idea that a woman that attractive would want to go out with him seemed absurd, she was way out of his league.

"Hey Ned," Rebecca said with that big smile that was just melting Ned's heart.

"Oh hey Rebecca," Ned said already feeling as though he were getting cold feet. Asking out a girl was always difficult for him but he knew he had to grow more of a backbone if he ever wanted to get anywhere with her.

"Hey Ned how's it going," she said still smiling and waiting for Ned to make the next move.

"Rebecca this may sound a little bit weird, but do you think maybe you would like to go out and do something sometime? Like maybe we could go out this weekend."

"Well I can't miss church on Sunday; I've always been really strict about that and everything. You could come to church with me if you want, I mean if you don't think a college-age girl being religious is kind of a weird thing, especially in California like this, well I understand."

"I have to admit that I'm totally not religious but I mean I am open-minded about these things."

Rebecca smiled. "Well not all religious people are Bible thumping fire and brimstone fundamentalists; I actually come from a very open-minded and very tolerant church. You're not going to see any kind of shaming or homophobia or sexism or anything like that at my church, believe me, it's a very progressive and open-minded kind of church."

"Well okay then, I guess I will see you on Sunday then."

"Great, I'll see you then."

Ned went back over to Jackson who high-fived him.

"I can't believe that she decided to go out with you," Jackson said.

"Yeah but it was just to go to church with her, so I'm not expecting anything wild or crazy to be happening. But that's okay, like I said I'm more than willing to take it slow, a little bit old-fashioned like that, so a girl like Rebecca is perhaps the ideal woman for me."

The rest of the week all that Ned could think about was the fact that he was actually going to be going out on a date with Rebecca. He didn't even care if it was going to some stuffy old boring church; just the fact that he was going to get to go out with Rebecca was enough for him to be on cloud nine.

"I don't really have that much formal dress wear," Ned said as he looked through his closet to look for some of his nicer clothing. "I just hope that there's not like a strict dress code or anything, I don't want to feel that I'm underdressed, but I really have mostly casual clothing. I don't want to make any faux pas that are going to ruin things with Rebecca."

He decided that he would just put on a nice jacket and outfit that he had, that should be good enough. Maybe it wasn't a suit and tie but it sounded like it was a pretty progressive church. He actually didn't know exactly what to expect at a church, as he hadn't been to any type of formal religion since he was younger, and didn't really have any formal opinion on spiritual matters.

Ned decided it was probably easiest to just meet Rebecca at the church, and as he approached the church he saw that it looked as though it were a pretty big church that must have had a fairly decent following. Outside he saw on the message board come as God made you, there is no shame in that.

"Hey Ned I'm glad that you could make it," Rebecca said as she approached. He was a little bit relieved to see that she was dressed rather casually, which made him feel better about the fact that he wasn't overly dressed up.

"I hope what I'm wearing is okay and appropriate for church because I really don't have much formal clothing," Ned said.

Rebecca laughed. "You are really silly Ned, didn't I tell you we don't care about things like that, and we are a very nonjudgmental and very open-minded church. Didn't you see our motto written on the message board outside?"

"Come as God made you," Ned said as Rebecca nodded. He couldn't help but smirk to himself because when he heard that he thought that God had pretty much made him naked, and he couldn't help but begin laughing a little bit.

"What's so funny?" Rebecca asked as she continued smiling.

"Nothing, I just sort of thought of a joke I heard, it's kind of an inside joke," Ned said shaking his head. He didn't want Rebecca to think he was some kind of pervert, although he didn't also want her to think that maybe he thought she was overly naïve simply because she was religious.

"Well come on, services are about to begin shortly," Rebecca said as they walked into the church as Ned saw a sign that said undressing room on it as Rebecca started heading towards it.

"What is the undressing room," Ned said as he stopped Rebecca.

Rebecca laughed. "Come on Ned it's pretty easy, just follow me," she said as he shrugged his shoulders and followed her.

Ned practically stopped in his tracks and did a double take as he saw men and women in the undressing room actually getting undressed as they slowly slipped out of their clothing and hung them neatly on hangers that were provided.

"What the hell," Ned said. "Sorry I didn't mean to swear in a church but, seriously what the hell?"

Rebecca laughed again. "I guess you have never been to this church before Ned, but that motto outside, as God made you, well maybe you didn't get the idea, but this is a nudist church."

"A nudist church," Ned said trying to look her right in the eye even as he found his eyes wandering to the fact that there were naked men and women around them hanging up their clothing casually like it were no big deal. At first he thought this had to be a joke, but as he looked at all of the naked people around him he was beginning to feel that being underdressed was something that was no longer something he needed to be concerned with.

"You don't have a problem with nudity do you," Rebecca said as she began getting undressed as Ned felt all of the blood rushing downward as his heart began beating.

"Seriously, a nudist church," Ned said.

"I guess I should have told you, I just didn't think that you had any problem with the human body or anything like that," Rebecca said as she finished getting undressed and hanging up her clothing as she stood there naked in front of him with her hands on her hips looking extremely comfortable with the fact that she was completely buck naked.

Ned didn't even know how to form words. He couldn't believe that Rebecca was standing there in front of him completely naked, her stunning body completely on display, as she was smiling and didn't seem the least bit embarrassed or awkward about the fact that she was naked.

At this point Ned couldn't disguise the fact that he had a raging hard on which made him suddenly feel self-conscious in spite of the fact that at the moment he was the only one in the undressing room who had not yet undressed as he began covering himself up.

Rebecca laughed. "You don't have to be embarrassed about that Ned, it happens, it happens a lot until you sort of get used to it. But there is nothing sinful or shameful about natural biological reactions like that, as God programmed our bodies to respond to beauty with excitement. You're not saying anything Ned, is everything okay?"

"It's just I have never been naked in a church before, or in public before for that matter," Ned said now feeling intensely embarrassed about the fact that he was standing there surrounded by naked people with a very obvious erection.

"Well I suppose there is a first time for everything," Rebecca said still smiling and looking completely not bothered by the fact that she was still completely naked.

"Hey Rebecca who's this, and why are they still dressed," another woman said as she came over who also had a pretty rocking body as far as Ned was concerned.

"Oh hi Lucinda, this is my friend Ned, and I think he's a little bit shy," Rebecca said.

"Nice to meet you Ned," Lucinda said shaking his hand, and he was trying his hardest not to stare directly at her cleavage and breasts, but it was very hard not to when they were all out on display right in front of him like that.

"Nice to meet you too," Ned said, hardly being able to form words and he felt that his hands were probably sweating, and that his pulse was probably racing and that Lucinda probably noticed.

"Anyway there's nothing to be embarrassed about, God made you the way he did and there is nothing to be ashamed of about that," Lucinda said as she started walking off, and Ned couldn't help but stare at her perfect ass jiggling up and down as she walked.

"Come on Ned, we don't want to miss the beginning of services," Rebecca said. "Do you need help getting undressed?"

"I'll be there in just a minute," Ned said as Rebecca nodded and left him there in the undressing room. Was he really going to go through with this, was he really going to get naked here in a church like that? He was glad that it wasn't a repressive church, but maybe it went a little bit too far in the opposite direction!

Ned took a deep breath and very reluctantly, very slowly, started getting undressed and hanging his clothing neatly on a hanger in the undressing room. He then took another deep breath and walked into the church where he could see that the pews were basically filled completely with naked people.

"Over here Ned," Rebecca said waving over to him as he took a seat next to her with their bare naked flesh touching.

Ned couldn't believe that he was sitting there naked in church between two very attractive naked women, and he was wondering if it would be considered a sacrilege if he accidentally blew his load right then and there. Ned knew that he must be blushing intensely.

"Hey Ned, you don't feel weird about this do you," Rebecca said as she could see that he was clearly shaking in the pews.

"No of course not, there's nothing wrong with being naked in church," Ned said laughing nervously and trying to convince himself as much of that statement as he was anybody else.

"Exactly," Rebecca said as everyone began facing forward but Ned couldn't help but have a wandering eye. He couldn't remember having ever seen this many naked people before. Not all were as hot as Rebecca by a wide margin but naked was still naked!

"Everybody please rise," the pastor said as he approached the podium which interestingly enough concealed his naked body from the parishioners.

Ned felt really reluctant to rise because he had already arisen in a certain area of his body that he was hoping that nobody would notice, despite how obvious it was. As he stood up with his erection pointing straight forward he found his eyes darting to the side to see if anybody was staring at him, as he couldn't remember the last time he had felt so utterly embarrassed but also so ragingly turned on, and in a church of all places!

The fact that the woman standing up in front of him had a really great ass that was inches away from that area of his anatomy that he was hoping that nobody would notice was certainly not making it easier.

The pastor than instructed everybody to hug the person next to them as Ned found himself hugging Rebecca and then hugging Lucinda, and this wasn't helping the situation. Having direct physical contact with naked female flesh was not going to make his erection go away anytime soon.

Once everybody had seated in the church Ned was surprised to find that it was a fairly standard sermon about charity and love and good work and not being judgmental. It certainly was a progressive church, none of that fire and brimstone stuff that had turned him off from religion when he was younger, but the fact that nobody seemed to be phased about the fact that they were naked made him feel really out of place there.

He also couldn't help but notice as his eyes wandered around the church that lots of the stained-glass and lots of the murals on the wall depicted men and women who were naked and seemingly not ashamed of it.

Finally when the church service was over Ned had actually managed to calm down a little bit but he knew that he hadn't stopped blushing, and he probably hadn't stopped trembling almost the entire service.

"So Ned what did you think of our church," Rebecca said smiling.

"Well it was certainly different from the way I remember when I was younger," Ned said. "In fact I can't even remember the last time that I was in a church."

"Well it's never too late to come back to God, he's always there waiting for you," Rebecca said still smiling, still not the least bit bothered by the fact that everybody could see her naked.

"I remember when I went to church as a child that the Adam and Eve story was kind of told differently, where Adam and Eve suddenly became ashamed when they realized that they were naked."

Rebecca nodded. "Well we have a different interpretation of the Bible here, here the story of Adam and Eve is rather different. Rather than being ashamed when God saw that they were naked God encouraged them to celebrate his creation. In fact one of the principles of our religion is that it is somehow sinful to hide what God has created. In our faith we believe, we have sort of a holy saying, if God had meant us to be wearing clothes we would have been born dressed. Obviously he has nothing that he wants us to hide, and in fact it would be positively sinful to hide ourselves when we don't have to if at all possible, as the human body is God's most beautiful creation, and he wants everybody to see his best work on display. You don't have to feel ashamed of being naked before God, he knows exactly what you look like already. I hope that someday society will become more understanding of our faith and allow us religious exemption to having to wear clothing in public."

"So you basically just spend all your time when you are not out on the streets completely naked?" Ned said.

Rebecca smiled. "Of course, I mean you don't stay dressed all the time do you?"

"I mean I get undressed in the shower, and you know if something sexual is going to happen."

"Our church doesn't consider nudity to be inherently sexual," Lucinda said as Ned once again started covering himself up. "I didn't mean that in the sense that we thought there was anything wrong with being sexual. You don't have to feel guilty Ned, just because you are appreciating all of the beautiful bodies that God has created all around you."

"Does it make me a pervert that I'm getting really turned on by all of the naked flesh on display," Ned said.

"It's just a little weird now because you aren't used to it, but if you come to the church regularly you will think nothing of it," Rebecca said. "You may not believe this, but at one time I was a little uptight about getting naked in church, but after a few services I realized that it was no big deal, and I'm sure that you will eventually realize that as well."

"Rebecca, Lucinda, it seems you have brought a new member to our church," said one of the female pastors said as she walked over, and once again Ned felt all of the blood rushing to his nether regions as she was far too attractive to be a pastor!

Ned immediately began covering himself up again as this was just mortifying.

"Don't worry about that, we don't judge people for things like that here, God created the male body in a way that things like that are only natural and shows that you appreciate the beauty of the female form," the pastor said. "I'm Luanne and I hope that you don't feel uncomfortable in our church."

Ned shook Luanne's hand and once again felt his hand was trembling a little bit. "I feel a little bit out of place, and I have to admit while you were up there giving your sermon it was a little bit difficult to concentrate on what you were saying."

Ned knew that now he was looking down at his feet and blushing but Luanne was just laughing.

"You know I get that a lot from new parishioners, personally I'm a bit flattered, I didn't really think that I was all that distracting," Luanne said as Ned tried his best not to stare at her breasts, but she had some pretty big ones, and he didn't know how any man in that congregation was able to look away from them. He had no doubt that she was probably one of the reasons a lot of people were going to church.

"Well I mean," Ned said once again finding it hard to find

words. He didn't know a polite way to say that her breasts were huge and walking around naked like that what was she expecting?

"Hey if what God gave me helps me get more people to see the light that is certainly nothing to be embarrassed or ashamed about," Luanne said once again laughing. "Anyway I was wondering if any of you would like to sing in the church choir."

"The church choir," Ned said. "You mean like up in front of everybody, singing in front of everybody, singing naked in front of everyone?"

Luanne nodded. "I guess some people are a little bit uncomfortable about the idea of speaking or singing in public."

"It's not so much the singing or the speaking part," Ned said as he felt himself fiddling with his thumbs trying to do anything to distract himself from the fact that he was standing there naked with three attractive naked women around him.

"Oh you are going back to the whole nudity thing again," Luanne said shaking her head. "It seems a lot of people get really hung up on that aspect, I never understood why, it's so comfortable to be naked. Well anyway I hope that you will think about it, as we always need more people in the choir."

As they all waved goodbye to Luanne they went back to the undressing room and got dressed again, and Ned had to admit that he felt a little bit more secure now that he had clothing on once again, like finding a life jacket while lost at sea.

"Anyway Ned we had a great time today, and I really hope that you will come to church with me again next week," Rebecca said. "Do you think maybe we could all join the choir?"

Now that they were wearing clothing again Ned could focus on something other than the fact that they were naked, although he found himself mentally undressing both Rebecca and Lucinda almost as soon as they were dressed again, as he certainly couldn't get that image out of his mind of what they looked like naked. He couldn't believe how casual they were about the fact that they were naked, about how he knew what they looked like naked.

The thought of standing up in front of hundreds of people completely naked and singing was an unimaginable nightmare of embarrassment to Ned, but as he stood there looking at Rebecca and once again picturing what she and Lucinda looked like naked, to say nothing of Luanne, he found himself gritting his teeth.

"You know Rebecca why not, let's all join the choir," Ned said.

"Great, I will sign us all up," Rebecca said, and just like that it was a done deal.

"So how did things go with Rebecca at church," Jackson said rolling his eyes. "She wasn't like one of those Holy Roller fundamentalists was she?"

"No, I think it was actually a very very very progressive church, very," Ned said.

Jackson smiled. "Well it's great that you had such a fun time at church, although I have a feeling that it's going to be a really long time before you see some type of church girl like that slipping out of her clothing for you. But hey you said you wanted to take it slow, so I guess that works out pretty well for you."

"Actually I joined the choir."

"You joined the choir; I've never heard you sing anything."

"Well hey, how hard could it be?" Certainly not as hard as he was when seeing all those naked bodies! "Besides Rebecca is actually a really great girl, and I met some of her friends at her church, and they were all really nice." Really nice and crazy hot and naked!

"Yeah but nice girls can sometimes be uptight girls."

"You know you are wrong about that, just because somebody is religious doesn't mean that they are uptight, let's just say when I said this was a very very progressive church I really meant it, and believe me Rebecca is certainly not uptight, I mean good God is she not uptight."

"Well dude it sounds like she's a keeper."

Later that night as Ned went to sleep and thought about Rebecca and her amazing naked body; he had to think to himself that Jackson was certainly right, she was a keeper. However as he went to sleep that night he also felt kind of weird at the thought that God was watching him when he was naked. Then he thought more awkwardly what if God were female and how much more awkward that would be. He kind of wondered what people at the church thought of that.

"Well Ned, God created us the way we are, so why should

we be ashamed of our bodies," Rebecca said at church that next Sunday as they started getting undressed.

"Well doesn't it seem weird to you that there is this all powerful being and they are watching you while you are naked?" Ned said.

"You know I had never actually thought about it, I guess I'm just not really self-conscious about those things. Why does the idea of something like that watching you make you feel kind of awkward? Because you know it shouldn't, I mean if there is an all-powerful being that created you in his image he certainly shouldn't be judging you for looking like he is, or she is. We tend to believe that God doesn't actually have a sex but that God created both of the sexes so that they can enjoy each other, enjoy each other's beauty, so that we could appreciate our bodies and the differences we have between them. I can appreciate your body; I hope you can appreciate mine."

Ned smiled. "Believe me Rebecca; I really really appreciate your body, whether clothed or unclothed."

"That's really sweet of you Ned," Rebecca said as she kissed him which gave him a warm tingly feeling throughout his body, his admittedly naked, vulnerable and exposed body.

Ned found that Rebecca actually was surprisingly spiritual about all of this naked stuff, to the point where she didn't even seem to think any of it was the least bit strange. Maybe he had been looking at things the wrong way. He always told himself that there was nothing shameful about the human body, was always very liberal on sexual matters, but social conditioning ran pretty deeply, and the idea of all of this uninhibited nudity was certainly a new sensation and experience for him.

As they took their places in the choir to begin singing Ned couldn't help the fact that he was still getting an erection seeing all of the naked women around him, but strangely enough as they began singing he started to focus more on, well the singing part! All of these people seemed to be extremely comfortable being vulnerable because they kept mentioning how when you believe in a higher power you have nothing to feel ashamed of, that being vulnerable is a sign of strength, not weakness.

As Ned, Rebecca, Lucinda and numerous other parishioners started meeting multiple times a week to practice in the choir, the strange thing was that Ned actually was getting used to the sensation of being naked in public. He still found himself blushing and getting excited, but the strange thing was as they focused on the singing amazingly sometimes even forgot that he was up there completely naked.

"You have all been doing great, this is one of the best choirs I have ever had the pleasure to teach," Luanne said. "You are all a testament to God's grace. And I hope that at the big midnight mass on Christmas Eve that you will have people packing into the pews."

Ned had to admit that the idea of a large audience was intimidating, but he figured that the chances of him meeting anybody that he knew were still pretty slim, so that made him relax a little bit.

"Hey Ned, long time no see," Jody, his ex-girlfriend, said as she ran into him one day.

"Oh Jody, hi, how have you been," he said feeling really awkward because they sort of left on bad terms. He never felt comfortable around Jody the way he did around Rebecca. Made because Jody was a little bit high maintenance, a little bit status obsessed, always wearing the fanciest clothing and jewelry and everything. When Madonna was singing the song material girl she was probably thinking about somebody like Jody.

"I've been pretty good, I heard that you're going out with some type of holy roller choir girl now," Jody said. "I never had you pegged as the religious type, although you always were a little bit uptight."

"Her name is Rebecca, and she's not some kind of fundamentalist, she is very open-minded and very comfortable in her own skin," Ned said perhaps not wanting to phrase the last line the way he did. In fact he had never met somebody more comfortable in their own skin than Rebecca, certainly nobody who felt as comfortable exposing her skin to the world as Rebecca. "We are actually in the choir together."

"So you're a choirboy now, wow," Jody said. "What church do you go to?"

"Why, are you thinking about joining?" Ned said rather sarcastically as he knew that Jody was certainly not the religious type, and if she knew that he was going to a nudist church she would never let him live it down.

Jody shook her head. "No I don't go out for all of that religion with their anti-materialism and holier than thou attitudes and all of that repression and misogyny."

"Not all churches are like that Jody, this is actually a very liberal, progressive and open-minded church, probably the most open-minded church I have ever been to, not that I have been to a lot of churches mind you."

"Well maybe I will have to look it up some time," Jody said snorting as she shook her head. "Anyway Ned have fun being a choirboy."

Ned had to admit that Jody always made him feel uncomfortable, and he was surprised that they lasted as long as they did. He felt that Jody was rather judgmental and a little bit snobby, although she was attractive, he wasn't going to deny that, and in fact he wouldn't have dated her if that weren't the case. He never thought that he was her type, and he never thought that he had a chance with her, but when he got the chance he wasn't about to turn it down as she was sort of a big woman around campus so to speak.

"Now Jody is the last person I would want to run into at church," he said shaking his head.

On the night of the big Christmas pageant where he would be singing in front of the largest audience he had so far, Ned was certainly nervous. Although he had somewhat gotten used to being naked in the choir like that he still felt intimidated the more people that happened to frequent the church.

"Are you ready to go out there and knock them dead tonight," Rebecca said as they got undressed in the undressing room.

"Yeah, we are going to really be great up there," Ned said, even though he had to admit that he was suddenly getting cold feet. However he promised that he would do this and he didn't want to let Rebecca down, so he swallowed his pride once again and forced himself to go up there in the choir.

The turnout was rather large as there was probably a lot of people who even at a naked church only went on Christmas and Easter, and it definitely seemed as though the church were packed, but seeing as everybody else in the church was likewise naked at least he blended in with the crowd, and that helped him to relax a little bit.

However about halfway through the whole production that was when he noticed somebody in the back of the church, someone who stood out for the fact that they weren't naked, in fact they were quite well-dressed. It was Jody, and not just Jody but she had her friends Justine and Amber who were likewise pointing at them and laughing and seemingly holding up their camera phones.

As soon as Ned saw her looking over in his direction with that arrogant look in her eyes and laughing at him, he suddenly started losing all of his confidence and was finding it hard to keep singing.

"Is something the matter Ned," Rebecca whispered to him as she looked over in the distance and could see that Jody and her friends were in the back of the church having a grand old time poking fun at all of the naked people. "Don't let them get to you."

Ned knew that Rebecca was right, but at the same time the fact that he was standing up there naked and making a fool of himself in front of his ex-girlfriend and her equally snobby friends was utterly humiliating beyond belief.

When the service was over Ned was quite glad to get out of there, and wanted to run right towards the undressing room so that he could put his clothing back on, until he noticed that Jody and her friends were blocking the way. He wanted to find some way to escape from this situation but he didn't see any way out of it as he saw Jody and her friends walking over with confident strides, and clearly not hiding the fact that they couldn't stop snickering.

"Well well well, when I heard you were a choirboy I certainly wasn't expecting this," Jody said as Ned began covering himself up and blushing profusely as Jody, Justine and Amber were barely able to contain themselves.

"Jody, what are you doing here," Ned said barely able to make eye contact with her.

"Well when I heard that you were going to a church and in a choir I looked up Rebecca's social media profile and could see that she was associated with this church, but when I realized what kind of a church it was, well God damn, how could I not check this out," Jody said as she laughed.

"Please don't take the Lord's name in vain like that," Rebecca said.

This was absolutely mortifying and Ned would have given

anything to get out of there.

"When I heard you were dating the religious girl like I certainly wasn't expecting this, not only is she not uptight she's a God damned exhibitionist," Jody said. "I always knew you were weird Ned, but wow a naked church, who in 1 million years would have thought that you would join a place like this? I mean aren't you ashamed of yourselves?"

At that moment Ned had to admit that he felt more ashamed than ever before, he could feel his skin crawling, and he knew that now he must be blushing like never before. The fact that Jody was having at him and he didn't have a stitch of clothing on her while she was covered from head to toe made his confidence drop down to about zero. It was easy for him to feel comfortable naked when everybody else was naked, but now that he was confronted with his ex-girlfriend standing there dressed and laughing at his naked body he just wanted to crawl into a hole and die.

"There's nothing to be ashamed of, this is just the way God made us," Rebecca said. "And it's the way God made you as well, because under our clothing we are all naked. It takes a person who is of deep faith to be able to just stand there naked before the world and to God."

As Ned saw Rebecca standing up for herself, getting right up in Jody's face like that, it was at that moment he realized why he liked Rebecca so much better than he liked Jody. He always thought that Jody was confident, even arrogant, but Rebecca was both humble and strong at the same time.

"You wouldn't have half the guts that Rebecca does," Ned said now making eye contact with Jody and trying not to shake too much over the fact that she was seeing every inch of him naked, as were Justine and Amber who were standing there snickering with her. "If you are so great, if you think you're such hot stuff, why don't you get naked like everybody else here?"

Jody sort of snorted but as she looked around to see that she and her girlfriends were the only ones in the entire church who weren't naked, but she was outnumbered and it seemed as though her confidence was faltering a little bit.

"As if I would become some type of stripper in a church, come on ladies, let's get out of here," Jody said walking off clearly uncomfortable as they stormed out through the undressing room.

"Oh Ned I'm so proud of you for standing up like that, proving that your faith was stronger than her insults," Rebecca said as she hugged Ned causing a wave of arousal to go through his body, but he managed to control himself.

"You know Rebecca I really mean it, you have taught me that it takes a lot of guts to allow yourself to be exposed and vulnerable like this, and I don't think I would have ever learned that I was capable of that if not for you," Ned said. "I can't believe I used to think that you were this uptight religious priss, and yet here you are probably the strongest woman that I have ever met, confident, unashamed and proud without being arrogant."

"Oh Ned now you're making me blush," Rebecca said and for the first time she actually looked a little bit uncomfortable, and actually was blushing, as Ned likewise blushed.

"Well hey as great as this all was maybe it's time for us to get dressed now," Ned said as Rebecca nodded and they went into the undressing room.

As Ned saw everybody else in the undressing room slipping back into their clothing he kept looking around looking for his own outfit, that jacket that he had been wearing for as long as he had remembered, everybody knew it was him when he was wearing that jacket, and that was when he realized something terrible.

"Jody," he said under his breath. As she was leaving she probably saw Ned's clothing on the hook there and decided to take it.

"Well looks like someone's getting less shy, you're the only one who hasn't gotten dressed yet," Lucinda said as she and Rebecca stood there in front of Ned as he began blushing again.

"It seems like your clothing might have been misplaced," Rebecca said as Luanne came back out once again fully dressed.

"Well it looks like somebody doesn't want to leave church," Luanne said. As Ned stood there as the only one currently undressed he once again felt extremely self-conscious in front of these dressed women.

He realized that there was probably no way out of this awkward situation so he simply smiled and laughed.

"What's so funny," Rebecca said.

"Well you said that in this church we dress the way that God made us, and I guess that God, in their infinite wisdom wanted me to stay dressed the way he made me," Ned said as everybody had a good laugh and he kept on laughing as long as he could, as that was probably the best way to forget that with his clothing having gone missing that until he found a resolution to this predicament that a lot more people were going to see him just as God intended.

"So how did things go with Rebecca at your big choir thing?" Jackson asked a few days later. "Have you seen her naked yet?"

Ned simply smiled and began laughing as Jackson simply shook his head and wondered what was so funny.

A Naked Gift underneath the Christmas Tree

Bethany was decorating the Christmas tree, and she had to say she did a pretty good job she thought as she stood there and admired her work.

"You know I think that I have finished decorating the Christmas tree, and there's nothing else that I think that I could add to make it more attractive," Bethany said.

"You know will be really attractive, you lying naked underneath the Christmas tree," her husband Paul said as he laughed.

Bethany had to admit that even though he meant to jokingly it actually was a pretty hot idea. Imagine him coming home on Christmas Eve and finding her sprawled out naked waiting for him underneath the Christmas tree. As she thought about it for the rest of the day she thought that the idea was really kinky, and she couldn't get it out of her mind, and then decided that what the hell, she might as well try it.

When Paul texted her that he was on the way home and that he had a very special surprise for her, she texted back that she had a very special surprise for him as well waiting underneath the Christmas tree.

As she got undressed and started lying down naked in front of the Christmas tree, leaning on her elbows in a really sexy come-hither way, she couldn't wait to see Paul's face when he walked in the door and saw her naked underneath the Christmas tree just as he had joked earlier. It would totally blow his mind.

"Bethany I'm home and I brought something very special for you," Paul said as he opened the door.

"I have something very special for you waiting underneath

the Christmas tree," Bethany shouted as she closed her eyes and began snickering to herself, only to open her eyes and see Paul standing there with her entire family who dropped everything that they were doing and were staring at her gap mouthed as she began screaming.

Bethany got up so fast that the Christmas tree went falling down as she scrambled to hide behind the couch.

"Merry Christmas," Bethany said as she tried to cover herself up and stood there blushing profusely and waving coyly to her family, who she was not expecting to see since they lived over 1000 miles away.

Once she got over the initial shock of what happened everybody had a good laugh about it and had a more or less conventional Christmas but as she was sitting in bed later with Paul they were both smirking.

"I have to say this was definitely a surprising Christmas for both of us, but there was something rather kinky about finding you underneath the Christmas tree all naked like that," Paul said as he smiled and kissed her. "You know I never would have thought of that, I'd love to be able to do something like that for you."

"You flew in my family as a surprise for me, and although it ended up being a horribly awkward situation I couldn't think of anything more thoughtful," Bethany said before smirking. "Although –"

"What do you mean although?"

"Nothing," Bethany said smirking to herself knowing that Paul was Jewish, and the idea of him getting naked to light the menorah eight nights in a row was kind of a sexy thought, she would just have to make sure that if he was going to do that that she wasn't going to surprise him with his relatives for the holidays!

<u>Some Words from the Author</u>

I always like to include a little word at the end of everything that I write about what inspired this and what I was hoping to achieve with a particular story, and I think this one pretty much speaks for itself. This is just a short CFNM novella that I thought would be funny about what if a woman wished on a shooting star that her boyfriend couldn't wear clothing for the entire Christmas holiday while they were in Hawaii, and inexplicably it ends up coming true and drives all of the humorous action of the story.

Once again I feel that the character Ethan is a little bit based off of me. I don't have phobias of flying or snakes or anything like that, but I sort of shy and awkward, especially in public, so once again I place myself in the role of this character and think what I would do in a situation like that. So it's another one of those situations where you have a character who is shy and awkward but because of weird supernatural forces is forced into awkward and embarrassing naked situations.

The character of Marissa was actually based on this girl that I knew in high school that looking back in retrospect I think had a crush on me but I was rather oblivious to it. Now I just sort of know her distantly on social media but she turned out to be a real estate agent, so this character was directly inspired by her and how I think that she would probably behave in a situation like this.

All in all I thought that it was just sort of a nice funny and kinky kind of holiday story about a woman getting her ultimate holiday wish, and her boyfriend eventually joining in the excitement and overcoming his inhibitions, and I think that it was sort of a nice little romance story about two people who are a little bit opposite but who somehow managed to get together in spite of that and are brought closer by the results of their awkward naked situation resulting from her holiday wish.

Since this was a relatively short book I wanted to include a couple of bonus stories from future collections of embarrassing naked stories that I hope to publish that have sort of a holiday theme. I came across about five stories that I think have sort of a Christmas theme that I think work rather well as bonus stories for this collection. The naked choir one I was on the fence about including seeing as it only has one part of it taking place on Christmas, but I thought it was a really good story, so I included it anyway.

So here a little bit of the author notes now for those remaining stories.

<u>My Night as a Naked Secret Santa</u>

This is one I just thought of off the top of my head, and it was the last thing I thought of before I started writing, but I figured that this would make a really good CFNM story, as I thought it had a really unique premise, and I figured that I might as well write a Christmas story for my naked collection.

All in all I can to say I am really happy with the way the story flowed from beginning to end. I thought it was a really original idea and everything, and then the way I thought about ending and I think worked out pretty well as well, because that was just as spontaneous as the rest of the story.

Our Holiday As Naked Christmas Trees

I really didn't think that this will be a really long full-length story, but I am glad that it turned out really well. I got this idea earlier today when I was watching Sabrina the Teenage Witch and she mentioned the idea of the Christmas tree being naked, and I just thought that that would be a great concept for a story, women who are naked Christmas trees! That was actually why I decided to name my main character Sabrina, which I think good because I never used that name in any of my naked stories before, at least I don't think so anyway, but maybe I did. But this wonderfully ended up slowing really good from start to finish for something that had just sort of a weird concept I managed to run with it, and like usual it basically writes itself.

Naked Underneath the Mistletoe

I wanted to write a crazy naked story for Christmas and I think that this story was pretty simple and straightforward, I just thought it would be more interesting that instead of kissing under a mistletoe what if people had to get naked under the mistletoe and spend the night together, waiting another great story of awkward and embarrassing nudity that ends up bringing two people together. This one contains naked in public, embarrassed nude female, embarrassed nude male.

The Way God Made Us: The Story of the Naked Choir

I think that this was a story that was a very long time in the making. Although I only thought of the story two years before I ended up writing it, I think that what really inspired it was that when I was young I read a magazine called Weekly World News, which is like the original fakenews, as they would make up things like bat boy and other crazy stuff, but I remember in one issue there was this article about a naked church where they had all of these pictures of people, albeit censored, being naked in church, and I think that that fired up my young imagination just as I was approaching puberty and stuck with me all those years. Then years later I actually found those images available online in archive of the magazine, and I think that that was probably where I got the idea for actually writing a naked story about it.

I wouldn't be surprised if there actually was some kind of church like this, and I thought it was an interesting story that explores the spiritual aspects of being naked and the human body and everything like that. I couldn't imagine myself in a church like that, but it would certainly be interesting, and it just shows that not all religions are necessarily repressive, in fact some go pretty far in the opposite direction, but in the end my characters managed to be open-minded and realized that they are better for each other than a lot of the other more narrow minded people in their lives.   It also makes a good point that if there was a God who created us in his image and meant us to wear clothing then why weren't we born dressed? It is similar to a story in one of my earlier collections called The Church of CFNM.

This story involves mutual male and female nudity, naked in public, embarrassed nude male, CFNM and CFNF.

A Naked Gift underneath the Christmas Tree

This was just sort of a really brief story that I thought of that I thought would make a good bonus story for my CFNM holiday novella and I guess there's not really that much to say about it. It's just a regular embarrassed nude female Christmas story I guess you would call it!

I hope you enjoyed all of the stories in this collection and if you did then fear not, for I have an almost infinite number of ideas for future stories along these lines, both short story length and novella length and longer. So someday there will be more. But if you have read this far you must have quite enjoyed them so I hope you'll give this book a good review. And don't forget to check out my blog at https://arthurhpemmington.blogspot.com/ for future stories and previews of my novellas and novels. I tend to post the stories there first and then when I have enough for a collection I release them as a book. So if you like the stories on my blog you will hopefully like the stories in future volumes as well.

Happy holidays!

www.ingramcontent.com/pod-product-compliance
Lightning Source LLC
Chambersburg PA
CBHW071335140726
47996CB00005B/1979